To, Susan Please Enjoy you L. Barnett Evans & C.V. Rhodes

SAVING SIN CITY

A Novel by

L. Barnett Evans
and
C.V. Rhodes

SAVING SIN CITY

Published by GRINCO, LLC
P.O. Box 781142
Indianapolis, IN 46278

This is a work of fiction. All events, characters, places and incidents are strictly products of the authors' imagination. Any similarities to persons living or dead are completely coincidental.

First Edition

ISBN: 978-0-9838614-2-3

CHAPTER 1

"We're going down!"

Hattie Collier screamed at the top of her lungs as she wondered how her simple need for change in her life had led her to this—crashing head first into Las Vegas. She didn't deserve to go out like this! Terrified, she waited for her whole life to flash before her. Instead all she could think of were the past few months that had lead to this ignominious end.

She was "sixty-something" years old, born and raised in Indianapolis, Indiana, and she rarely traveled outside of its confines. Hattie had married her high school sweetheart, Leon, and had been blessed with a happy union for thirty-five years. Now a widow, she still lived in the first house that and she and her husband had bought as a young couple and it was filled with most of the furniture that they had purchased over the course of their marriage. Nothing was new.

Yet, one morning she had awakened and decided that she needed a change in her life. It wasn't because her life wasn't already full. She had her two children, and four beautiful grandchildren. She had good friends and, of course, she had the Lord. What more could she possibly need or want? The only answer she was able to come up with was that she needed more.

For those who knew her, the fact that she was considering any changes at all in her life was the equivalent to a tornado ripping through the Midwest or a hurricane hitting the Florida coast. Hattie Collier was not a woman whose life was conducive to change. Yet, she hadn't questioned the revelation. As far as Hattie was concerned the only explanation for this metamorphosis was the Lord. He was talking to her and she always obeyed His will. So she had sat down and made a list of changes that she planned to make in her life and the first was the ultimate act of independence. Hattie had become an entrepreneur.

The name of her business was Half Way Home. It specialized in offering the bereaved personal assistance in planning a king's burial on a pauper's budget. Hattie was a firm believer that the dearly departed had a right to go out like super stars. No one could dispute her expertise when it came to funerals because Hattie Collier was a professional mourner.

She couldn't count the times that she had attended the funerals of people that she didn't know. If she found a name in the obituary section that listed few family members, she felt that it was her God-given duty to see the poor soul home. That's how the idea of Half Way Home was conceived and in the short time that she had been in business she'd already had thirty-one referrals.

Her two best friends, Bea Bell and Connie Palmer, had been shocked when she went into business for herself, but they had been supportive. That's how it was with the three of them. It was their code of friendship. They could fuss, argue, insult each other and disagree vehemently, but at the end, they had developed an unbreakable bond.

Half Way Home was on its way to becoming a success, so Hattie had decided that it was time to begin looking like the new woman that she was becoming, and while she was at it, take care of some of the other changes that she wanted to make in her life.

On the day she decided to tackle her new look she started her morning as usual by kissing Leon good-bye. He had been dead for quite some time but his picture was still sitting in its gilded frame on top of the fireplace mantel in the living room and the kiss had become a daily ritual. Tucking the list of changes in her purse, she headed to the bus stop.

She walked with the same graceful stride that had attracted Leon when she passed him in the halls of Crispus Attucks High School so many years ago. She had been a leggy five foot eight inch beauty then and she was still attractive. The daughter of a minister, Hattie had never worn makeup, then or now. Her dark brown complexion was nearly free of age lines and her soft brown eyes were framed by long, lush lashes. Over the years she had made no concession to enhance her physical appearance. Even her mode of dress remained the same. She had always been conservative in what she wore. Pants were out of the question. She always wore dresses or skirts, dark in color, with collars and long sleeves. Her purses were plain, her shoes were practical. She was a consistent woman.

Hattie fought pride and vanity constantly, but that was difficult to do when it came to her hair. She had always had beautiful hair. In high school it had been coal black and hanging down her back. Her late husband had loved her dark tresses and was dismayed when she had her hair cut into a loose shoulder-length bob. That had been over twenty-five years ago and she hadn't changed the style since. Now her hair was silver-gray, but as thick, soft and silky as it had been when she was a girl. Yet, this was a new day and she was headed for the beauty parlor with the hope of looking like a brand new woman when she emerged.

The bus came to her stop. She stepped onboard, flashed her bus pass and took a seat. Hattie had never learned to drive. She had been a housewife all of her life and had depended on her husband for transport. After his death her sense of independence had grown with each passing year and she had learned to maneuver the bus lines.

Getting off the bus in front of a beauty shop that she had passed recently, she glanced at the name on the door—Total Eclipse. That seemed appropriate. She planned on her physical metamorphosis eclipsing anything that she had done to date.

Three hours later, Hattie left the beauty parlor buoyed by the compliments of its patrons. If she had to say so herself she looked good. Now it was time to go to a department store and purchase an entire new wardrobe. With that pending purchase, her goal of a complete makeover would have been achieved. That would leave two things on her list to accomplish. She wanted to learn to drive, and the very last entry, settle things with Reverend Trees. Hattie blushed.

She meant no disrespect to her late husband's memory. She would always love Leon, but for years there had been an unspoken attraction between her and the pastor of her church. Finally, she was going to do something about it. She didn't know how, but she knew that with the Lord's help she would figure out a way.

No, Hattie Collier was not a woman whose life was conducive to change, but she had finally stepped into the 21st Century when she boarded the plane with Bea and Connie. Going down on an airplane headed to Las Vegas before all of her goals had been reached had not been on her agenda!

****

Bea Bell wasn't ready to die in any airplane crash either. When they got onboard, she had familiarized herself with each exit and she was glad that she was sitting one row away from the door. When the aircraft lurched and Hattie's shouted warning vibrated throughout the cabin, she reassured herself of her survival, Lord willing, and mentally planned her escape. Over the years, she's had her ups and downs, but the ups had been winning lately and she wasn't going down without a fight.

As far as Bea was concerned, she had gone through enough in her life and she deserved to survive. Fifteen years ago she had lost her husband of thirty-two years, leaving her a widow. That had been tragic enough; but, it was the death of her elder son, James, Jr., some years later that had nearly destroyed her.

A rare form of cancer had taken her child in the prime of his life. She thought that she would never recover from his death, but fate had brought a miracle into her life. A few years ago she had been reunited with Frank Schaffer, her high school sweetheart, and just when it looked as though they might enjoy a future together, he had died suddenly.

After that Bea couldn't image ever being truly happy again. She had become content with her life. She had the love and devotion of her youngest son, her granddaughter, and her dear friends. Some people didn't have that. Yet, sometimes life has its own agenda, and the unimaginable can occur in the strangest places. For Bea it happened at the checkout counter in a grocery store.

She had been standing at one of those self-service checkout registers that she hated. She preferred human contact; but the checkout lines were long. So she opted for the alternative and things were going pretty smoothly at the mechanical monster until she was stopped by the bulk item in her cart—a bunch of greens. Having identified the picture of the item, she was trying to figure out the code to enter for the price when a sexy male voice resonated behind her.

"You punch the numbers into the pad there."

Bea turned to thank him and her knees nearly buckled. Smiling down at her was one of the finest specimens of manhood that she had seen in quite a while. He appeared to be in her age range, without a beer belly and with a head full of hair. All she could do was stare.

"You punch the code in here," he repeated. Reaching across her, he pointed to the machine.

Once again, his words were met with silence. Bea's brain had stopped working. She couldn't move or speak. He didn't seem to notice as his eyes scanned the screen and he punched in the code for her. The price appeared instantly. Bea wanted to sink into the floor and it had nothing to do with the machine.

"Th…thank you," she managed to stutter.

"Think nothing of it." He stepped back into line behind her.

Embarrassed beyond belief, Bea quickly bagged her purchases, inserted her cash for payment, retrieved her change and all but ran toward the exit. She didn't look back. All she wanted was to get out of there and put the humiliation of having been struck speechless behind her.

As Bea packed the car she wondered why the sight of a good looking man left her so tongue tied. The same thing had happened when she was first reunited with Frank. What was there about such men that made her act like a complete fool? After all, she still looked pretty good. Maybe she wasn't the svelte little cheerleader that she had been in high school, but at five foot two she wore her one hundred and fifty pounds well. Her round, caramel colored face was still devoid of the age lines that ravaged those of other women her age. She was stylish and sophisticated, and her shapely legs were still impressive.

In her younger days, she had been a real head turner. She could still swivel a couple of them even now. Decades of marriage had eroded the confidence of youth, but she was getting better at the witty repartee and the subtle flirting that she had to relearn after becoming a widow. Still, in spite of her progress, she found that when she was really attracted to a man, common sense seemed to elude her. It was counter to the strong, confident woman she knew herself to be.

Before she retired as a top administrator in state government, Bea had worked with some of the most prominent people in the city of Indianapolis. Her influence had reached from the Governor's mansion to the average man on the street. She still had contacts that she could use to her advantage if needed, to say nothing of the fact that her son, Bryant, was a detective in the city's police department. Living vicariously through his career had given her an excellent nose for sniffing out crime and corruption, that and a natural talent. This being the case, she could say with pride that her self-confidence had rarely been in short supply.

Preoccupied with that thought, she slammed her car trunk down and turned to take the grocery cart to a corral. Just as she did her cart collided with another shopper's cart hitting it hard enough to nearly topple it over. Bea jumped, startled at the impact.

"I'm so sorry!" She cried, turning her attention to her victim. To her astonishment it was the hunky helper from the grocery store. Bea froze.

"No problem." He looked amused as he righted his cart, preventing his groceries from spilling.

Seeking escape, Bea turned abruptly and without another word got into her car. She had been humiliated twice today. What else was there to say? Through her rearview mirror she noticed the man hesitate for a moment and then head toward his car. Bea pulled out of the parking spot and out of the lot.

As she drove toward home, she berated herself for her cowardice in not indicating her interest in him. She vowed that it would not happen again. The next man who piqued her interest was going to experience the full force of Bea Bell's charm.

****

Connie Palmer squeezed the hand of the man next to her as she waited for the oxygen mask to fall from its place. If she was going down at least it would be with the man that she loved. She sneaked a glance at David Austin. He looked undisturbed.

That was David. He walked through life with the courage of a lion. In that arena they had a lot in common.

Connie had always plunged into life without fear, and she wasn't afraid of death either. She considered it as inevitable as the success that she had enjoyed in her life.

Born in a small southern town, she had dropped out of high school and married her childhood sweetheart, Robert, when she was sixteen. Fearlessly, the young couple had moved to the city of Indianapolis without knowing a soul. They had worked hard, purchased a house that they could not afford and then with very little capital they had established Palmer Realty. Her company now owned rental property all over the city and although Connie lived modestly, she was a very wealthy woman. Like her friends, she was in her sixties and it had never occurred to her to vegetate just because she had reached a certain age. There would be no retiring for her.

Connie and her two friends had even formed an informal detective agency which they called Grandmothers, Incorporated. That venture had been the result of having investigated the unexpected death of Bea's old high school sweetheart, Frank Schaffer. At the time the ladies had suspected his estranged wife, Charlie Mae, in his death. Bea and Charlie Mae had been rivals since high school and Bea had been hell bent on proving her nemesis guilty of Frank's murder. The result had been a lawsuit filed by Charlie Mae against the three of them for slander. The suit was still pending.

In Connie's opinion it should have been that heifer Charlie Mae getting ready to meet her maker in an airplane crash instead of Connie and her friends! How ironic it would be if the good news that she had delivered to Bea and Hattie a few months ago would result in such a tragic ending.

She recalled the day that she told her friends about her good fortune. David had been there with her when she received the news about winning the drawing that would put them all on this airplane. He was the first one with whom she shared the news. After all he would be one of the people reaping its benefits.

She had met David Austin years ago when she had hired him to manage her properties. At the time it was strictly business, but she had found him attractive with his sparkling dark eyes and coffee brown complexion. Their business relationship had turned into a friendship that had gradually evolved into a personal relationship. David was her lover—her secret lover. None of her friends knew about him. She and David had been discussing that issue as well as a few others the day that she received the telephone call about Vegas.

He had stopped by her house unannounced as she was dressing to go out. The light banter had turned into a heavy conversation when David brought up a subject that Connie would rather have avoided.

"When are you going to make an honest man out of me, Mrs. Palmer?"

It was a question that he had asked Connie often.

"Don't start, David," she warned as she slid into a blouse and then started to walk past him. David caught her arm and gently turned her to face him.

"I've told you a thousand times, baby. We need to do the right thing. If it's the age thing, you know that it doesn't bother me. It's not like we're teenagers. I'm fifty years old. If I don't know what I want by now, there's no hope for me."

"David!" She had tried to retreat, but he wouldn't let her.

"I know it can't be about money. I've got plenty of my own. I've never asked you for a thing…"

"David, please…"

"Are you ashamed of me?"

The question stunned her. "Of course not!"

"Are you sure? Do you think it's lost on me that after all of this time I haven't met one of your friends?"

Connie winced. He was right.

"Well, I plan on changing that."

"Oh, really?" He sounded skeptical.

Connie felt badly. "I'm sorry, David. I know that I haven't introduced you to my friends, but, believe me; I'm not ashamed of you. I've just been selfish. I wanted someone all to myself that I didn't have to share with anybody else, but I've been wrong. It's hurt you. Now it's time to show you off." She hugged him to her.

"Humph," David had said flatly, trying not to look pleased by her declaration. "So you're going to parade me around like a monkey, I suppose?"

Pulling back to look into his face, Connie saw through his charade. "That's right. You look too good for me to do anything else."

He smiled. "Then when's the unveiling?"

"Hummm," Connie tapped her finger against her lips as if in thought. "I think I'll do it at the Charity Auction. You'll look real good dressed up in a tux."

David protested that decision. He hated black tie events and last year he had avoided this one like the plague. Eventually, she convinced him to be her escort this year and she yelped in delight as he sealed the deal with a slap on her rump and a kiss. That's when the telephone rang and she learned the good new.

As she called Bea to tell her what had happened she thought about her talk with David and realized that their discussion had been the nudge that she needed to do right by him. The Charity Auction would provide a great opportunity to do even more than merely introduce him to her friends. She wanted some of the important people in her life to get to know each other. That's what made the surprise that she had for her best friends so great.

She could hardly contain her excitement as she urged Bea to get Hattie on a three way.

"I hope you are two sitting down," Connie had gushed breathlessly, "because do I have something to tell you. A little while ago, I got a call from the Midwest Realtors Association and they informed me that I had won a seven day, round-trip, all expenses paid, trip for four." She had squealed, "Ladies we're going to Las Vegas!"

It had been those words that had put them on this flight to Sin City. They had looked forward to this trip, and Connie had been happy that she could be the one to offer it to them. It further solidified the bond between the three of them.

She had come late into the friendship already established by Bea and Hattie. The two women were Indianapolis natives and had grown up in the same neighborhood. They had graduated from Crispus Attucks High School together and had been bridesmaids in each other's weddings.

Connie and Bea had met when Bea's oldest son, James, Jr., dated and eventually married Earlene, the second of Connie's four children. It hadn't taken long for the two mothers to become close, especially after their granddaughter, Tina, was born. The two women worked together in supporting Earlene as a single parent after James' death. They were good grandmothers, as was Hattie. It was through Bea that Connie and Hattie had met.

As their husbands died, leaving all three women widows, the friendship between them had strengthened. They each had become intricately entwined in each other's lives. Now it looked as though they might be ending their lives together.

CHAPTER 2

Hattie was close to hyperventilating. It was true that she wanted to see her Lord and Master, but did it have to be today? She was in the prime of her life! Surely the Lord didn't need her right now. He had been so good to her over these past few months. Why should all of that good be wasted? Of course things had been a bit shaky in the beginning, but this trip to Vegas was supposed to change all of that.

Her makeover had been a major hit in the salon. Hattie had hardly recognized herself, but she was apprehensive about what her mother-in-law, Fanny Collier, would say when Hattie walked into the house sporting her new hairdo.

Of course Miss Fanny's first reaction had been overly dramatic. She had clutched her chest and wailed, "You cut it! A woman's hair is her crowning glory!" That had been something that her son Leon had often repeated.

Already tentative about her decision, Hattie's insecurity had surfaced at her mother-in-law's words. She had turned in a circle to give Miss Fanny the full effect of her stunning feather cut. It tapered at the neck and framed her oval shaped face perfectly. A silver gray rinse had been added, offering shiny highlights that accentuated her dark complexion.

"Don't you like it?" she had asked, anxiously. Despite their contentious relationship, the older woman's opinion did matter to her.

Miss Fanny studied her from all angles before she answered.

"To tell the truth, you look better than you did when you were married to my son. I just can't figure out why you waited until he's been dead all these years to spruce yourself up. Leon was always saying how beautiful you were. I just chalked it up to the fact that love is blind. But, I can truly say, you do look good."

Hattie had been stunned. Her mother-in-law's words had brought tears to her eyes. That was one of the nicest things that she had ever said to her. The woman had been sniping at Hattie since the day she and Leon had started going together. Miss Fanny had never considered her good enough for her only child. Yet, despite that,

Hattie had done her Christian duty and taken the old crone into her home. After all Miss Fanny was family and the grandmother to her two children; but, it did seem that at times the Lord was testing her when it came to the woman. It was a test that she was determined to pass, but she wasn't Job! So the words of praise from Miss Fanny were doubly special considering the source and after clearing that hurtle, it was the reaction of her two best friends that she was anxious about. The three of them were to meet the next day at an upscale restaurant to celebrate the trip to Vegas and Miss Fanny volunteered to drive Hattie. In doing so she had inadvertently invited herself to dine with them.

When they entered the posh interior of the restaurant, Hattie spotted Bea and Connie across the room and gave a small wave. She watched as Bea's smile of recognition which was aimed at Miss Fanny turned to one of confusion as her eyes shifted to Hattie.

Bea squinted and then took her glasses from her purse and put them on. Her eyes held a million questions as the tall, attractive figure in the fashionable dress and the familiar face framed by a stylish hair cut approached the table. Bea turned to Connie, but she found her to be equally transfixed. When Miss Fanny and Hattie finally joined them, all Bea and Connie could do was stare.

"Hattie?" Bea couldn't believe that this was her lifelong friend.

"Yep, it's me." Hattie was overjoyed by her reaction.

Bea shook her head in an effort to absorb what she was seeing. She turned to Miss Fanny.

"Hattie?" She needed confirmation.

Miss Fanny nodded. "It's her in the flesh."

Getting up from the table, Bea circled her friend. She touched her hair, her dress and then stepped back to take in her entire appearance. "You look beautiful!"

Tears filled both women's eyes as they embraced. Hattie was touched beyond words. Between the two of them, Bea had always been the swan. Hattie had never expected to receive such praise from her.

"Hattie, you do look beautiful," Connie agreed breathlessly.

"Thank you." Hattie swallowed the lump in her throat. Connie was the fearlessly candid one among them. Her word was bond.

Miss Fanny intervened. "I'm sorry to interrupt this admiration society, but I'm hungry. I hope that you two don't mind if I join you."

There were no objections and the waiter took their orders. While the ladies waited for their meals to arrive Connie asked Hattie the question that all of them wanted answered.

"Why? What made you do this?"

"Connie, for years you've been trying to hammer into my head that the only constant in life is change." She patted her hair. "I finally decided to give it a try."

"I'll say." Bea was still in shock. "And you did it with a vengeance."

Nobody at the table could disagree. Hattie's startling transformation was the topic of conversation until their dinners arrived. The subject then turned to the progress of the lawsuit being initiated by their mutual enemy—Charlie Mae Shaffer.

"The cowardly hussy wouldn't dare show her face in court to testify against us," Bea spat contemptuously. The woman who in high school had stolen the man that she had planned on marrying was going down.

"I don't think that you'll have to worry about her anymore," Miss Fanny gave a smug smile. The others turned puzzled looks her way.

Miss Fanny shook her head in disgust. "Don't you great detectives ever read the newspaper?"

The women continued to look confused. Miss Fanny didn't keep them in suspense.

"It looks like Charlie Mae is going to be too busy for any law suit." There was a twinkle in her eyes as she paused dramatically. "According to an article that I read in the paper this morning, Charlie Mae, Charmaine, or whatever she's calling herself these days, might be going to jail."

Three pairs of eyes blinked in disbelief. Miss Fanny pulled a copy of the newspaper from her purse and with great fanfare set it in the center of the table. Connie was the first to reach for it. She read the headline: Real Estate Mogul Suspected of Tax Fraud! She read the story aloud about how real estate maven, Charmaine Schaffer was under indictment for tax evasion and mail fraud.

"Looks like the heifer is gonna get her comeuppance," Hattie gloated. "The Lord don't like ugly."

"Amen to that." Bea couldn't stop grinning. This was turning into one twenty-four hour period that none of them would soon forget. Connie won a trip to Vegas, Hattie emerged as a swan and their annoying nemesis might be spending time behind bars. How much better could life get?

The four of them had clicked their glasses and toasted to their good luck. Now as the airplane continued to shake and rattle it looked to Hattie as though that luck might have run out.

****

Trying to avoid panic regarding her present situation, Bea chose to remember the day that Josh came into her life. She had been at dinner with her friends celebrating the trip to Vegas, when she noticed Connie glancing over her shoulder. A smile of recognition creased her face as she watched someone across the restaurant.

Noticing Connie's distraction, Hattie had followed her line of vision and nearly choked on her glass of water. "Oh, my goodness"

Miss Fanny echoed her sentiment. "Good Lord!"

Curious about what had elicited such a reaction from the ladies, Bea was about to turn to see its cause when suddenly a man was standing behind her. From her vantage point she couldn't see his face, but she certainly could smell his cologne. It was all male, just like the timbre of his voice.

"Connie Palmer, I thought I recognized you."

"Why, Josh. It's good to see you." Connie smiled up at him. "It's been years since I last saw you. What are you doing in town? "

"Believe it or not I'm closing the Las Vegas office and I'm opening one in your fair city. I'm living here now. I'm even building a house."

"How nice!" Connie was all but drooling at the gorgeous hunk grinning down at her. He had that same effect on most women. A glance at Hattie and Miss Fanny confirmed that observation. She could see that they were dying for an introduction, and Bea was itching to turn around to see who was causing such a stir. Connie did the honors.

"Joshua Pierce, I'd like you to meet my friends, Mrs. Hattie Collier…"

Josh shook Hattie's hand, "Mrs. Collier."

"Mrs. Fanny Collier"

Josh bowed slightly and shook Miss Fanny's hand.

"And Mrs. Beatrice Bell."

As Josh stepped around so that he was facing Bea, she blinked and then blinked again. Before her stood about 6-foot, 3-inches of honest to goodness Hershey chocolate bar, sporting a silver mane to die for and a smile that could cause cardiac arrest. She knew that as a fact because it had nearly stopped her heart the day before. This was the man from the grocery store.

"Nice meeting you, Mrs. Bell." His eyes sparkled with recognition as he extended his hand.

She shook it as the unspoken attraction stood silently between them.

"Nice meeting you, Mr. Pierce," Bea managed to croak.

"I'm glad that I ran into you," Joshua returned his attention to Connie.

Reaching into his expensive sport coat he withdrew a sterling silver card case. He handed a linen business card to Connie.

"Let's get together some time."

"Of course." Connie took the card from him and withdrew one from her purse and returned the gesture. "The annual Real Estate Charity Auction is coming up soon. It's a major fundraiser for the local realtor's foundation. I'm selling tickets. If you're interested in attending, call me."

"I certainly will." Backing away, his eyes swept the table. "And I hope to see you ladies again." His eyes lingered briefly on Bea. "Have a nice evening." He walked away.

The four women grinned like hyenas as their admiring eyes watched his departure in appreciation.

"Uh, uh, uh," Hattie grunted. "The Lord sure knew what he was doing when he made that one."

"You can say that again," Connie agreed, surprised at Hattie's reaction. She was usually so reserved.

"You three need to act your age," Miss Fanny grumbled as she savored her steak dinner, "You act like you've never seen a man before, especially one like that." She gave them a salacious grin.

Fanning herself with a napkin, Bea didn't try to disguise the interest in her voice as she addressed Connie, "You have three seconds to start telling me about that man. Where have you been hiding him?"

"Well, I'm glad to see that you've finally awakened from the dead," Connie teased, delighted at her friend's interest. "I told you that you need to…"

"Connie," Bea warned. "I am not interested in another lecture about how long Frank has been dead and how I should move on with my life."

"Okay then." Connie got the message. "I met Joshua at a realtor's convention in Las Vegas a few years ago."

"Is he the one you came back raving about how nice he was?" Hattie remembered that Connie had been glowing with praise.

Bea had noticed that Connie looked uncomfortable. It wasn't until later that she found out that it had been David Austin that she had been talking about.

"Uh, no, Josh is a housing contractor, a very rich one. He got his start in Las Vegas. The last time I talked to him his Midwest office was in Columbus, Ohio, but from the sound of it he's opening another one here in Indianapolis."

"Is he married? Attached?" Bea wanted the important facts.

"As far as I know, he's still single, unless something has changed. From what I've heard, he's never been married."

"You're kidding!" Hattie was shocked. "You don't think that he's one of them happy men, do you?"

"Happy men?" Knowing Hattie's penchant for misstatements, Bea took a moment to think about her meaning. "Do you mean, gay?"

Connie came to the rescue. "No, he's not gay. It's my understanding that something happened in his past, a personal tragedy of some kind, and that's why he's never married."

"He sure is good looking." Hattie nearly purred. "And he was doing some looking at Bea."

Bea started. "What?"

"Oh, he was looking all right," Hattie teased. "Didn't you notice, Connie?"

"No, I didn't," Connie answered.

"That's because you were too busy ogling and gushing," Miss Fanny sniffed.

Connie took the ribbing lightly. "Like you weren't"

"We all were." Bea couldn't calm her excitement.

"No lie about that!" Hattie wiggled her brows.

Connie chuckled, "Well, look at you, Hattie. When did you become so observant about the opposite sex?"

"You told us that all you needed in your life was Jesus," Bea reminded her.

"Maybe this is part of this new liberating life change she's been yakking about," Miss Fanny observed.

Hattie gave them a mysterious smile. "A little something else in my life won't hurt." With a wink, she picked up her glass of water and drank.

"Okay, Miss New Woman," Bea quipped. "But he might have been looking at me because we met yesterday at the grocery store." She proceeded to tell them about her earlier encounter with Josh Pierce. "I never thought I'd see him again."

"It must be the Spirit at work." Hattie was a witness to that power.

"All I know is that if there's another opportunity to meet him I'm making my move."

"I know that's right." Connie gave Bea a high five. "Speaking of which, we need to discuss the trip to Las Vegas."

"Yes!" Bea pumped her hand in the air with delight.

However, Hattie was as reserved as she had been when Connie had first broken the news.

"Don't they call that place Sin City?" She gave a disapproving frown. "Why on earth would we want to go there?"

"To have fun, Hattie." Bea wasn't going to let this woman tamper with her euphoria. "We'll be doing something different."

"Come on, Hattie," Connie pleaded. "This trip is important to me."

"I don't care whether she comes or not," Bea announced. "Count me in."

"And if she don't want to go, I'll take her place," Miss Fanny piped in.

The other ladies looked at her in surprise. Hattie's frown intensified.

"Miss Fanny, you're too old to go to Las Vegas. What would people say about you wandering among a den of sinners?"

Miss Fanny put her fork down and looked Hattie squarely in the face. "I don't give a rat's behind what people say. If God gives me the strength to go I'm going! So count me in, Connie."

Once again the ladies had raised their glasses for a toast, with the exception of Hattie. Cavorting with sinners was not on her agenda. It hadn't been on Bea's either, but neither had crashing. If the Lord would hear her prayer, she wanted to see Josh again. She wanted the magic that they had found with each when they had gotten together to continue and there had been magic.

CHAPTER 3

Connie had called Bea and informed her that Joshua Pierce had contacted her and purchased a ticket to the Real Estate Charity Auction. Bea had vowed to herself that if she saw him there she would make a move on him or die trying. She could hardly wait until the evening of the auction, and not just because she wanted to see Joshua.

The Charity Auction was Connie's pet project and every year her friends supported her efforts. A couple of years ago, Connie had informed them that she had taken stock of her life and had concluded that she hadn't done nearly enough to give back to her community. Her husband and she had always donated generously to charity, but she felt that she could do more, especially in the area of education.

Connie had always been fascinated by the immense pride that Bea and Hattie had in their alma mater, Crispus Attucks High School. It had been established in the 1920's to segregate the races, but the result had been the development of a learning environment in which the seeds of success had been deeply sown and cultivated. Crispus Attucks had been a towering example of what could happen when young people were encouraged to do their best, in spite of the odds.

It was for this reason that Connie had organized the annual Realtors Charity Auction. The funds from this event not only awarded grants and scholarships to deserving students, but it also provided monetary awards to schools for equipment and supplies. Connie was proud of what had been accomplished over the years, and she worked hard to make sure that the auction was a success each year.

Bea knew that like her, Hattie was looking forward to the event as well. It was to be the grand unveiling of her new look. There would be people there who had yet to see her metamorphosis. She had purchased a dress for the occasion which neither of her friends had yet seen. For the first time in her life, it seemed that Hattie planned on getting a lot of attention. She would be the bell of the ball. However, Bea only wanted one person's attention and his name was Joshua Pierce.

On the evening of the affair, the swank ballroom where the Real Estate Charity Auction was being held had all the glamour of a Hollywood opening. Designer gowns and classic tuxedos abound. Tables were laden with succulent delicacies, while a live band offered musical entertainment as patrons enjoyed themselves on a dance floor. In a roped off section of the room rows of satin chairs faced an elevated podium, designating that as the auction area.

Bea saw Hattie and Miss Fanny enter the elegant ballroom and survey the swanky gathering. They were looking for her. She signaled to them.

"Connie outdid herself this time," Hattie said as they joined Bea at their reserved table.

"She sure did," Miss Fanny agreed.

Bea gushed with pride at Hattie's appearance. Her friend wore a silver, form fitting floor length gown that revealed curves and a bust line. Bea had never seen Hattie wear anything so perfect for her figure, and the sleek hairdo framing her face was the crowning touch. Bea couldn't say enough about Hattie's new look.

"My friend you look simply stunning this evening."

"Thank you. So do you," Hattie returned the compliment.

Bea was pleased by her comment. Dressed in a yellow, silk gown, accented with gold beading, Bea's hair was twisted in a stylish French roll. Diamonds sparkled in her ears and around her neck. She was the essence of sophisticated beauty.

Miss Fanny, who thought that she looked pretty good herself in a sparkling floor length gown, groused, "Let's eat."

They followed her advice and moved toward the serving tables. As they did so, Hattie's gown shimmered beneath the ballroom lights. She had never worn anything as daring in her life. The bodice was cut in a scooped-neck design. Her arms were bare. She had splurged on a pair of diamond earrings and a diamond tennis bracelet. As she glided through the ballroom, she looked and walked like a queen.

Bea teased. "You are aware that vanity is a sin, aren't you?"

Hattie smiled. "God forgive me, but I don't care. I feel good tonight."

"And you look just as good as you feel," Bea told her. She felt the same way about herself.

A tuxedo-clad waiter guided them back to their table. They had just settled down to enjoy their goodies when Connie walked up to greet them. She looked lovely in an off the shoulder Dior gown and she was glowing. As her friends looked from her to the handsome man draped on her arm, it was easy to see why.

"Hi ladies, I've been looking for you. I've got someone I'd like you to meet." She bestowed an ethereal smile on her escort. "This is David Austin. David, these are my friends Bea Bell and…" She paused, her eyes widening at Hattie's appearance. "And, I think this is Hattie Collier. I know this is her mother-in-law, Mrs. Fanny Collier."

David gave them his most engaging smile. "How do you do, ladies?"

The smile worked. The women were charmed as they turned curious faces toward Connie. She ignored their silent questions as she addressed Hattie.

"You're really wearing that dress, girlfriend!"

Hattie couldn't get enough of the compliments. "Thank you."

Bea gestured around the room. "It looks like a great turn out, Connie."

Her friend nodded. "I'm so excited. We've broken last year's record. Everybody who is anybody is here—the mayor, a couple of state Congressmen and Senators. You name it, they're here. Have you previewed some of the items that were donated for auction? They're fantastic. I hope you're planning to have a good time tonight."

"Looks like you do," Miss Fanny speculated eyeing David.

"Yes indeed." Connie tightened her hold on his arm. All eyes were on her as the ladies tried to determine the situation with her escort and Connie knew exactly what their looks meant: *Girlllllll! We've got to talk!* They certainly did, but at the moment she had a job to do.

"Listen, ladies, the auction will start shortly, so I've got to get going. We'll see you later."

"Nice meeting you." David said following Connie toward the auction area. Her friends stared at them until they disappeared into the crowd. Bea was the first to break the silence.

"Well, I'll be!"

Hattie concurred. "I'll say."

"Sweet Jesus!" Miss Fanny groaned, drawing the attention of her companions.

"What's wrong with you?" Hattie admonished, thinking that her reaction was to David. "I thought he was nice and he certainly is handsome."

"I'm not talking about Connie's boy toy," Miss Fanny corrected her assumption. "I'm talking about the Queen Cobra slithering across the floor."

Hattie and Bea followed Miss Fanny's line of vision. They froze.

"Charlie Mae Schaffer," Hattie hissed, "and she's dressed to kill."

"That would be redundant," growled Bea. "The cow has nerve showing her soon to be jail bird behind in public! Pretend you don't see her."

"Too late," Miss Fanny drawled. "She's headed this way to show off. I can't believe the heifer's got two men on her flabby arms." She leaned forward with interest. "And the one on her right looks mighty familiar."

Hattie squinted. Her eyes widened. She grabbed Bea's arm. "One of the men is the one that we met at the restaurant, the one who knows Connie."

Bea's head snapped up. Her breathing nearly stopped. He was there. The time had arrived.

"It is him!" Hattie's voice rose in excitement. "It's Joshua, Joshua…"

"Pierce." Bea's voice quivered.

"But what in the world is he doing with Charlie Mae?" Hattie wondered.

"Looks like we're about to find out," Miss Fanny crossed her arms tightly. "She's headed straight toward us."

Draped in a chinchilla fur, Charlie Mae stopped at their table. Her smile was venomous.

"Hello, ladies. I'm surprised to see you here at such a pricey affair; but I guess it could be fun watching people with money spend it." Before they could respond, Charlie Mae turned to her two companions. "Let me introduce you to my two handsome escorts. Joshua Pierce, I'd like you to meet…"

"Mrs. Bea Bell, Mrs. Hattie Collier and the lovely Mrs. Fanny Collier," he acknowledged all three but his eyes strayed back to Bea. "It's good to see you again."

Charlie Mae was taken aback. "You know each other?"

The look on her nemesis' face was worth every erratic beat of Bea's heart. She tried to remain calm under Joshua's scrutiny. She had promised herself that she wouldn't retreat when she saw him again, and she didn't. Returning his gaze she noticed for the first time that his eyes were hazel and that the smile that he gave her was dazzling. Was that a dimple in his right cheek? She hadn't noticed that before either, but she had noticed his beautiful, silver gray hair. It complemented his complexion. She had also noticed that he kept in shaped—no beer belly thank goodness. His tailored tuxedo fit his toned body well. The man was fine! But, the man was with the wrong woman.

Joshua answered Charlie Mae's inquiry, "The ladies and I met a short while ago."

"Yes, Charlie Mae, on the same day that your fraud scheme hit the newspaper," Miss Fanny chided. She was delighted at having wiped the smile off of the woman's face. She turned back to Joshua. "It's a pleasure seeing you again, Mr. Pierce."

"Thank you, Mrs. Collier."

"Widow Collier," Fanny flashed a flirtatious grin.

Visibly upset, Charlie Mae raised her chin defiantly and turned to her second companion. "Max, this is…"

"Bea Bell, I heard." The shorter of the two men stepped forward. "I knew that I'd see you again."

Bea looked puzzled. Charlie Mae looked shocked. "You know him too?"

Bea couldn't testify to that. She studied the man trying to make a connection. He looked to be in his sixties, stood around five feet eleven and had a protruding belly that strained against his red cummerbund. Despite that and his thinning gray hair, he wasn't bad looking. Still, she couldn't recall him. He tried to assist her.

"It looks like I'm going to have to jog her memory a bit. Here's a hint for you: your telephone is ringing."

Bea continued to look at him blankly. Her mind was racing for a clue. Then, miraculously, there was a spark of recognition. This was the man that had pestered her at a wake during the time that she and her girls were investigating Frank's death. The one in the cheap suit whom she had nicknamed—

"Mr. Polyester." The name had slipped out inadvertently. "I...I mean..."

"Maxwell. Maxwell Anderson," he corrected her. "We met..."

"At the Feathers' wake," Bea finished the sentence.

Maxwell chortled with pleasure. "Aw, so you do remember."

Bea wanted to say barely, but she simply smiled. Maxwell turned his attention to Hattie.

His eyes sparkled with interest. "And once again, who are your charming friends?"

Noticing the man's interest in Hattie, Miss Fanny wasted no time speaking up, "I'm Fanny Collier and this is my daughter-in-law, Hattie Collier. She's a widow too." She nodded toward a humiliated Hattie. "All three of us are widows." She raised a suggestive brow. "And now that the introductions are out of the way, I want to ask you two, what are you doing with her?" She indicated Charlie Mae.

Thoroughly enjoying Miss Fanny's impertinence, Hattie and Bea held their laughter as a tight-jawed Charlie Mae maintained her cool façade. "I'll have you know that Maxwell is my escort for the evening. He is also one of the premier antique dealers in the city. Who better to help me find a treasure tonight? As for Joshua..."

"Mrs. Schaffer and I just met when she and Max came into the ball room," Joshua directed his comment at Bea. "Max and I have known each other for years."

"Oh really," Bea's spirits lifted. Joshua did have some taste after all. The three ladies gazed at the pretentious Charlie Mae in amusement. She had come to their table to show off, but she had been busted.

Charlie Mae hooked arms with both men. "The auction should be starting shortly. We had better look for a place to sit." Her voice was tight. Her anger was barely contained. Miss Fanny added more fuel to the fire.

"Since you're alone, Mr. Pierce, why don't you join us?"

The invitation had its intended effect. Charlie Mae was seething. Her façade was cracking. "We're going to find our seats now and..."

"Yes, do join us," Bea the Bold spoke up. Her smile solidified the invitation.

"Actually, I think I'd like to take the ladies up on their offer." Pointedly, Joshua removed Charlie Mae's hand from his arm. "Why don't you and Maxwell go on?"

The man's message could not have been clearer. Still, Charlie Mae was about to protest when Connie's voice came over the loud speaker inviting everyone to the auction area where the bidding would shortly begin. Charlie Mae gave a triumphant grin, but it was Maxwell who spoke up.

"I guess we'd better get on over there, but Josh, do come and join us." His pleading eyes met those of his friend's as he relayed a silent message. "Please." It was clear that he didn't want to be alone with Charlie Mae.

Josh seemed torn as he considered his friend's silent plea and then he looked back at Bea. He gave a sigh of regret. "All right, Max, if you insist." He turned back to the ladies making no effort to be coy. "Mrs. Bell, maybe we can get together some time."

Bea didn't hesitate as their eyes held. This was the perfect time to practice her new assertiveness. "Perhaps after the auction, and please call me Bea."

Joshua nodded. "I'd like that."

"We've got to go." Charlie Mae snapped. Grabbing Joshua's arm, she pulled him and Maxwell away from the table.

"Bye, Charlie Mae," Miss Fanny dismissed her with a wiggle of her fingers. "I'll see you in jail on visiting day."

"Not likely," snapped Charlie Mae, "But I will see the three of you in court. And my name is Charmaine."

The ladies watched with delight as she walked away in a huff. The table was just about to explode in laughter when they noticed that Joshua had abandoned his companions and was heading back to their table.

"Oh my, God!" Bea muttered, flushed with excitement.

"You've got you a live one," Miss Fanny whispered to her out of the side of her mouth just before Joshua stopped in front of Bea.

"Mrs. Bell… I mean, Bea."

"Yes?" She hoped that he couldn't hear her heart beating.

He flashed that smile of his. "In case we miss each other after the auction, may I have your telephone number?" He withdrew a card and a gold plated pen from his inside jacket pocket and handed both to her.

"You certainly can." Bea tried to steady her shaking hands as she scribbled her number and then handed the card and pen back to him.

Joshua pocketed both. "Thank you." Once again he walked away.

Bea fell back in her seat and began to fan herself frantically. "Lord have mercy. I can't believe this!"

"I can't believe it either," Hattie admonished. "I'm shocked by your behavior. You don't know that man!"

"She will," grinned Miss Fanny. "And from the look of it, very soon. Good for you, Bea, that is one good looking man."

"Yes, he is," Hattie acknowledged. "But for all Bea knows, he could be some sort of axe murderer or something! Good looks don't mean he's a good person."

Bea wouldn't be deterred. "You're not raining on this parade, Hattie. I haven't been so attracted to a man since Frank."

"I say, go for it," Miss Fanny encouraged. "As for you, Hattie, you've got an admirer of your own to worry about. Didn't you see the way that Maxwell fellow looked at you? I'd bet my social security check that he's gonna dump Charlie Mae and seek you out before this night is over. "

"I hope not," Hattie had recoiled at the very idea, but what she had seen in Maxwell Anderson's eyes couldn't be denied.

Bea agreed with Miss Fanny. "She's right, Hattie. You're looking good, so why not enjoy the benefits." That's exactly what she planned on doing when it came to Joshua Pierce.

CHAPTER 4

Gripping the arms of her airplane seat as if her life depended on it, Hattie knew that she should have been thinking about life and death, but instead she was thinking about the look that had been on Reverend Tree's face when he saw her with another man. She hadn't planned on that happening, but the Lord works in mysterious ways, and it was the events that followed that had lead to her being on this flight of doom.

The night of the Charity Auction, she and her friends had ended the evening at Connie's house. David had acted as host and he had been a hit with everyone. Neither Hattie nor Bea understood why Connie had kept her relationship with him a secret. They were disappointed that she hadn't confided in them earlier, but glad to have finally met him.

Bea and Joshua had met after the auction as planned and he had joined her at Connie's house that evening. Bea had been floating on cloud nine ever since. However, the same couldn't be said about Hattie.

While Joshua and Bea were at Connie's house, he had received a call on his cell phone from Maxwell Anderson. After he had taken Charlie Mae home, Maxwell had called to ask Josh about Hattie. When Bea told Hattie about the call, she was less than enthusiastic.

"After all, he was out on a date with Charlie Mae Schaffer," she reminded Bea. "What kind of taste could he have?"

Despite that Bea had talked her into going out on a double date with Josh and her, but Hattie had been reluctant. That being the case, the telephone call that Connie received the day of their big date should have been expected. Bea had put the call on speaker phone. She sounded deadly as she spoke to Connie.

"You had better talk to Hattie Collier or I'm going to kill her."

"What now?" Connie gave a frustrated sigh. She was sure that Hattie had gotten cold feet and refused to go. She was right.

"We haven't been on a double date since high and school and she is driving me out of my mind!" railed Bea. "I've been going through changes with her since she said yes to Maxwell. Now we're dressing, the guys will be here at six, and she's got the nerve to say that she's not going!" Bea grunted. "I'm getting ready to hit her in the head with a chair."

On the other end Hattie responded. "Connie, I'm trying to get this bonehead to understand that I am a woman in her sixties…"

"So am I," Bea countered.

"And I have been with only one man in my life."

"And I haven't?"

"Well you did have Frank." Hattie raised a knowing brow. As her best friend, Bea had confided everything to her about her relationship with him—everything.

Fuming, Bea gave Hattie the evil eye and left the room. Satisfied that Bea had been neutralized, Hattie returned to her conversation with Connie.

"I can't betray, Leon, and go out with another man! I thought I could, but—"

"Leon is dead, Hattie." An unsympathetic Connie put diplomacy aside. "He has been for a long time so let him go."

Hattie had expected to receive a bit more empathy from Connie. Her husband, Robert, had been her whole life. At least he had been before David Austin came along.

"Just because you've replaced your dead husband with another man does not mean that I'm going to do the same."

"Watch your mouth," Connie warned. "Don't say something you might regret."

Hattie measured her next words carefully—almost.

"Well, you're different from me, Connie. You don't care if you go to hell. I do. To me, marriage is forever. I want to do something different in my life, but not this. I just can't!"

"Then don't." It was obvious that Connie wasn't going to indulge Hattie. "All I can say is that at this stage in your life you're healthy, financially secure and very attractive. You're in a position that most women our age would die to be in. Yet, here you are complaining because some man finds you desirable enough to want to get to know you. Excuse me, but I find it hard to feel sorry for you. So, don't go out with him. I don't give a damn! Maybe he can go find somebody who will be grateful for his attention. Meanwhile, I mean to live my life to the fullest until they put me in the ground. Good-bye!"

Stunned, Hattie listened to the disconnect signal. "Well! I guess she told me."

"I sure hope so," Bea said in passing as she continued to get ready for Joshua's arrival. "I'm excited about this evening, and thrilled to have you and Maxwell along. I had hoped that having another couple along might calm my nerves…"

"But I don't know how to date," Hattie moaned. "All I know is how to be married."

Bea reassured her. "I'm not an expert either. After Frank, it never occurred to me that I would get another chance to go out with a man that I like so much—especially someone like Joshua."

Hattie smiled. "He is a cutie pie."

"Yes he is, and he's so nice," Bea gushed. "We've talked on the telephone until the wee hours of the morning getting to know each other. Now I'm going out with him and I have qualms. Hattie, we're both getting ready to wade into unfamiliar waters, and I'm just as scared as you are, but I'm willing to try."

Earlier Hattie had also been willing. As she and Bea got ready, the two of them had been like school girls—fixing each other's hair, helping each other pick outfits, laughing and giggling at the possibilities of what lay ahead, but as the time for their dates drew near Hattie's excitement had turned into anxiety until, finally, she flatly refused to leave the house with Maxwell Anderson. That had prompted the telephone call to Connie, and her friend's last words caused Hattie to think.

Over the past few weeks she had gone through so many life changes that she was beginning to wonder if things weren't getting out of control. Change wasn't easy. Yet, she had vowed to herself that she would try. Still, this going out with some man that she didn't know was so unlike her. She didn't recognize herself. She was a cauldron of emotions, and fear was the most prevalent.

What had possessed her? Why couldn't this date be with Reverend Trees? He was the man whose name that she had put down on her list. She knew that he liked her and she liked him too. He was her minister, and they were familiar with one another. Maxwell Anderson was an unknown. He was more of a distraction then anything, but, Connie's words haunted her. *I mean to live my life to the fullest until they put me into the ground.* That had been her own unspoken vow when she decided to make changes in her life. She wanted to tackle her fears and overcome them. Had she been lying to herself?

No! She hadn't. Squaring her shoulders, Hattie looked up at Bea. "I need you to pick out a perfume for me to wear for this evening. If I'm going to act like a Jezebel, I might as well smell good."

Bea had cheered Hattie's bravado, but that had lasted for about two hours, just long enough for the two couples to get to the five-star restaurant in which they were to dine. Once there Hattie had fled to the ladies room.

As she stood looking in the mirror at the hair, the dress, and the little bit of eye shadow that she had allowed Bea to put on her upper lids, she had to admit that she did look good. So why was she hiding away in the bathroom instead of sitting at the table with the first man she had dated in decades?

"Coward!" She admonished the woman in the mirror.

"Yes you are." Bea had entered the room and she did not look happy. Hattie couldn't meet her eyes.

She came to stand next to Hattie. "You were doing perfectly well when they picked us up and on the ride over here, but as soon as you saw Reverend Trees you came running in here like some scared jack rabbit. You've been in here fifteen minutes, Hattie. This is embarrassing."

"What is the reverend doing here?" Hattie couldn't have been more surprised if the Lord himself had made an appearance at the restaurant. He had been sitting at a table with three other men when they entered and he looked up and saw her. She would never forget the look of shock on his face. His eyes had strayed from her to Maxwell and then back again. A shaken Hattie had acknowledged his greeting as she followed the others to their table. Sitting with her back to the reverend, she could feel his eyes on her and she had tried hard to listen to Maxwell's constant chatter during dinner, but her mind kept drifting back to Reverend Trees. His presence, plus her ineptness as a date, had sent her fleeing to the ladies' room.

"Why he is out there is irrelevant," Bea answered her inquiry. "The question should be what are you doing in here?"

"I don't know what to talk to Maxwell about." She knew that she was lacking when it came to demonstrating social skills with the opposite sex, but she hadn't been aware of how truly pathetic she was.

What made it even more pronounced was that Maxwell was so affable. Sure, he dressed like a colorblind pimp. The green suit he wore tonight was in stark contrast to the conservative gray one that Joshua sported; however, Maxwell did have a sense of humor. But, he wasn't the reverend. That was another strike against him, that and the fact that he talked too much. He thought that he knew everything, and modesty wasn't a word with which he was familiar.

At the moment, Bea didn't care to hear any of her excuses. She too was upset.

"You left me out there to entertain two men," Bea complained, "and I don't appreciate it."

Hattie raised remorseful eyes. "I don't know what to do or how to act."

"Oh, and I'm an expert?" Bea snorted.

"At least you've been out with men before."

"I haven't had that many dates, Hattie, and this is different. Joshua is different. I find myself tongue-tied when I talk with him, but despite that I have managed to conduct some sort of conversation and if I can do it, so can you. I never would have abandoned you like this and I resent it. You accepted Max's invitation. If you don't like the man tell him that you don't want to see him again, but at least you could be polite."

Hattie nodded. "You're right, and I'm sorry."

"I hope you are. Max is talking my ear off. I want to talk to Joshua."

Hattie smiled. "I bet you do. He's a winner."

"He sure is and you're not helping by leaving me with Mr. Polyester."

"That's a good name for him. Maxwell does work that material." Hattie laughed for the first time that evening. "When I saw that suit he's wearing I figured that we won't need a green light on the public streets tonight."

Bea grinned and patted Hattie's shoulder reassuringly. "Don't worry about it. Seeing you with Maxwell is good for the reverend. Now that he thinks that he has competition maybe he'll get off his butt and do something about it. Anyway, you don't have to concern yourself about him being in the restaurant anymore. He left with his party about ten minutes ago. As for Maxwell, if you speak up and say something then maybe he won't dominate the conversation so much."

Hattie lifted a brow, "Do you think?"

"Yes, try to come up with a subject that you know something about."

Hattie nodded thoughtfully. "I'll try, that is if he shuts up long enough for me to get a word in." They headed toward the exit.

"Find an opening and out talk him." Bea opened the door and motioned for her to proceed. "I know you can do that."

Encouraged by Bea's pep talk, Hattie rejoined the men at the table and searched for a topic to discuss with Maxwell—something of interest, something that she knew a lot about. Turning toward him, she smiled.

"Did you know that Peterson's Funeral Home is offering 10% off coffins until the end of next month?"

From that moment on, Hattie found her voice and a topic of conversation—funerals. The evening ended with Maxwell escorting her to her door, then scurrying back down the walk like a man escaping from prison. Hattie had watched his retreating figure with a satisfied grin.

That evening had bolstered her confidence. To that end, her resolve had become absolute. The unspoken attraction between Reverend Trees and her was going to be settled once and for all.

Hattie's opportunity to come face to face with the reverend came sooner than expected. It happened the day after her date with Maxwell.

Having conducted business for Half Way Home most of the morning, she had arrived at her house feeling exhausted and looking forward to relaxing in a nice hot bath. However, it wasn't to be. As she entered her living room, much to her surprise Reverend Trees was sitting there being entertained by Miss Fanny.

Her mother-in-law had made herself scarce quickly, leaving Hattie alone with the reverend. He was as clean as the Board of Health, dressed in a navy blue suit, a crisp white shirt and a blue tie. His Stacey Adams shoes were polished to perfection and the cologne he was wearing was enticing.

"Why are you here, Reverend Trees?" She was surprised, but delighted by his presence.

He didn't mince words as he returned Hattie's unwavering gaze. "I came to see you."

The gauntlet had been tossed. The heat between them had begun to simmer and Hattie's trip to Vegas was meant to stir the pot.

CHAPTER 5

Connie glanced at the stewardess hurrying down the aisle. She didn't look panicked, but some of the comments coming from her fellow passengers indicated that they might be. Time seemed to have stood still since Hattie had screamed her warning. Connie wondered what she had been thinking. The woman could be a real nut case sometimes. She had proved that many times over the years, and especially when it came to Reverend Trees.

Hattie's friends had guessed long ago that the reverend was the object of her affection and they teased her about it unmercifully. Now, due to her recently self-declared liberation she had become serious in her pursuit of the minister. Yet, when she came face to face with the reality her confidence had faltered. That didn't seem to be the case with the reverend, especially after seeing her out with another man. He hadn't wasted any time asking her out, and of course Hattie had said yes.

The date was the weekend following her date with Maxwell, and Bea and Connie had been recruited to help her find something to wear. Her plan had been to scour her own closet for an outfit, but her friends had a surprise for her. They had gotten together and purchased a new outfit for her from an upscale clothing store.

"It's hot to trot," Connie gushed as Bea and she unveiled the ensemble. Grinning proudly, they waited for her reaction and of course it was as they expected.

"Oh, my God! That's for a Hoochie Mama!" Even with her new attitude, she never would have purchased anything like this.

The jacket and pants—she never wore pants—were made out of some kind of flowing material, and both pieces were flaming red. The jacket was knee length and the blouse—

"Oh, my goodness!" She was too through. "That thing is black and sheer, with a v-neckline. You'll be able to see the curve of my upper bosom."

"Let's hope so," Connie said brightly.

"Thank the Lord there's a jacket to cover up." She was mortified just looking at the thing.

"Oh that's not all of it." Bea revealed another shopping bag. This one was from Victoria's Secret.

"Surprise!" She whipped out a push up bra. "This is going to help those puppies travel north."

"And these," said Connie digging into the bag, "will encourage him to travel south." She extracted a pair of lace bikini panties.

"Help me, Jesus!" Hattie nearly fell off of the chair she was sitting on.

"And if he does it right, that's what you'll be shouting." Connie wiggled her eyebrows suggestively.

"Demon seed!" Hattie formed her fingers into a cross and aimed them at Connie. "I know this sinful looking underwear was your idea. You need salvation Connie and you're dragging Bea down with you." She stared daggers at the two sisters of Satan. "You two know good and well that I'm not going to wear any of this."

"Why not?" Bea looked at her innocently. "I think that it would look nice on you."

"Don't play with me, Bea. You two must have lost your minds. That outfit is not appropriate to wear on a date with a minister, and you know it." Rising from her chair, Hattie walked to her closet. "I've bought a lot of nice new outfits over the past few months and I plan on wearing one of them."

Connie and Bea exchanged glances. They had expected this resistance and had concocted a plan. Without a word, the two of them tackled her as though they were professionals in a wrestling league. Snatching the robe she wore off of her body, they pushed and pulled until they had dressed her in the clothes that they had purchased, although they did pass on the panties and bra. No matter how close they were as friends, neither one of them had a desire to see her boobs or her bare behind.

Hattie had never been so outdone in her life! She tried to protest, but her efforts proved futile. It was two against one. Before she knew it she looked like a red peacock. The ladies tried to put eye shadow and mascara on her, but Hattie thrashed and turned so much that they abandoned the effort.

"I'm not going out with a minister and I'm looking like a street walker!" she protested.

They did manage to put lipstick on her, dismissing Hattie's complaint that her lips looked like large, ripe cherries. Bea concluded the makeover by brushing Hattie's silver gray tresses until they gleamed. By the time it was over, Bea and Connie were sweating as though they had run a marathon.

Hattie was incensed, that is until she saw the results.

"Whoa! I thought that I was looking good the night of the auction, but baby." Her girls had done her proud!

"You're gorgeous!" Connie thought that the compliment was well deserved.

When the doorbell rang, Bea and Connie hid in the dining room and watched the action clandestinely as Hattie opened the door.

"Hello." She greeted him with her best smile.

The look on Reverend Tree's face was priceless. He complimented her so profusely that Hattie asked him to stop.

Connie and Bea had waited at Hattie's home until she came back from her date. As soon as he walked back to his car, Hattie was unceremoniously snatched from the front door into the living room where she stood face to face with Connie and Bea.

"Tell us everything!" Bea insisted.

"We want details." Connie demanded.

Still in a daze from her evening with the reverend, she couldn't wipe the smile off her face, but she did have an announcement.

"Ladies, I am going to Las Vegas!"

That was how she had informed her friends that she had changed her mind about going on the trip. Mysteriously, it seemed that all of a sudden Vegas had become more appealing.

****

As Hattie said what she assumed might be her last prayer before the plane went down, she couldn't get the reverend off her mind. She should have been thinking about her children or her grandchildren, but it was her one and only date with him that dominated her thoughts. It had been glorious, an evening that she couldn't forget.

His compliments had swept over her like a gentle breeze on a soft summer night. How often did a woman her age garner such praise from a man?

At dinner and at the art gallery opening they attended afterward, he had been attentive. Hattie had been thoroughly impressed. He had looked very nice that night, dressed in a conservative gray suit, white shirt and a gray printed tie. As a date he turned out to be charming, witty and a good conversationalist. Hattie had enjoyed the evening so much that by the time Reverend Trees took her home she had forgotten that she was suppose to be nervous, that is until they reached her front door. There they stood face to face, neither of them knowing quite what to say or do. Hattie's heart had been beating so wildly that she thought that she might be having a heart attack. Yet despite her anxiety, she hadn't felt so comfortable with a man since Leon. She never thought that she would enjoy such a feeling again. The reverend had been a perfect gentleman. He made her feel beautiful. He made her feel special, and she wanted him to know it.

"Reverend Trees…"

"I've asked you to call me, Samuel."

Hattie shook her head. "I'm sorry. It just seems funny calling you by your first name. I've called you Reverend Trees for so long."

He gave her an indulgent smile. "I understand." He took a step closer. "Now what is it that you were going to say to me?"

Hattie opened her mouth to speak, but her mind went blank. He was standing a little too close. For the life of her she couldn't remember what she was going to say. He had told her on the day he came to her home that after seeing her with another man at the restaurant he hoped that he hadn't blown his chance to let her know how much he admired her. Now she wanted to say something about how she felt about him, but she was tongue-tied. She took a step back. He took a step closer. Lord, have mercy! She wondered if he was going to kiss her. Leon had been the only man that she had kissed in her entire life.

Abruptly, she turned and, with key in hand, she had fumbled for the door lock and missed it completely. Help me, Lord! With shaking hands she had tried again. The key wouldn't fit in the lock.

"Need help?" Reverend Trees sounded amused.

"I think I can get it," Hattie muttered. Embarrassed, she couldn't look at him. Her aim was finally precise. She jiggled the key in the lock. Nothing happened.

Reaching across her, he removed the key and reinserted it. The door opened without incident. Hattie wanted to slip through a crack and disappear. She didn't. Taking a fortifying breath, she turned to face him. If a new woman was emerging the time and place was now. There were things that had been left unsaid for far too long. It was time to change that. She took a breath of courage.

"Rev...Samuel, I've admired and respected you for a long time, and tonight I've had the time of my life. I want you to know that I really like you. I really do, but I haven't had but one man in my life and that's my late husband, so it's hard, but ...but…" She eased back into the doorway.

"But what?" His tone was hopeful.

"But…" The sentence wasn't finished as Reverend Trees' lips met hers. The kiss was soft and tender. Slowly, he drew away.

"There are no buts, Hattie Collier. The annual church convention is being held in Las Vegas this year…"

"Las Vegas," Hattie echoed.

"Yes, and I have to leave in a few days to make final arrangements for the convention opening, so this might be my only chance to kiss you before I go." He did it again, just as tenderly but a little longer this time before drawing away. "Goodnight."

Reverend Trees retreated to his car, while a stunned Hattie stood rooted. It was then that she had decided that if he was going to be in Las Vegas, she would be there too.

After that evening, Hattie had begun a relentless campaign to get back the free airplane ticket that Connie had given to Miss Fanny. She had solicited Bea's support in her endeavor.

"You know the old sinner is going to go there and lose what little money she has," Hattie complained to Bea. "I'm trying to keep her from doing that."

"Hattie, what do you want from me?" snapped Bea. "I don't have time for your foolishness."

"Foolishness? I'm trying to help the woman," Hattie replied, making an attempt to sound earnest, "and you sound like you're ready to bite my head off."

Bea had been unsympathetic and Connie had been unyielding. Still, Hattie was persistent. She had been determined to be on this plane when it headed west. Well, she was on it and now she had to live—or die—with the consequences.

"Oh Lord!" Hattie wailed loudly as the airplane dipped again. "Have mercy!"

She really wanted to live and to get to that convention.

CHAPTER 6

Bea groaned in frustration at Hattie's latest outburst. As much as Bea loved the woman, her histrionics were getting on her nerves. As she sat with her eyes closed, trying to block out all of the confusion around her, Joshua Pierce continued to dominate her thoughts. She was so glad that he had come into her life. If she recalled correctly, Hattie had called her house harping about the ticket to Las Vegas that had been given to Miss Fanny on the evening of Bea's second date with Joshua.

"I can't find a single thing to wear," Bea had told her impatiently. "That's my priority, not the sob story that you brought on yourself. Joshua said that we were going out to dinner and to dress casual, but I don't know what that means. What's casual to one person may not be the same to another."

"Where are you going to eat?' Hattie asked changing the subject. It was obvious that she wasn't going to convince Bea of anything this evening.

"I don't know. He just said that we'd be dining out." Bea was rummaging through her closet. "And I'll be doggone if I'm going out not dressed right."

Hattie chuckled. "You're the only person I know that has every closet in her house stuffed with clothes but you never have anything to wear. Just calm down, I'm sure that you've got something that will do just fine. You're just nervous."

Bea bristled at that observation, not quite sure why she was so defensive. "No, I'm not! It's not like this is my first date with him. I just don't have anything to wear."

On the other end, Hattie shook her head. She knew this woman like a book. "Yes you are nervous. You like this man more than you're willing to admit, Bea, and you're scared of your feelings. You don't want to invest your heart in this relationship and get hurt again like you did when Frank died."

Bea was impressed by her friend's insight. She was right.

"It's just that all of this seems to be happening so fast. We've been seeing each other nearly every evening for a couple of weeks, but still I don't know him that well."

"I know, but don't worry about it. Say a prayer. Calm down and enjoy the evening."

Bea took a cleansing breath. "I will and thanks a lot."

"No thanks necessary." Hattie said sincerely. "Now back to that ticket to Vegas, I know that Connie called you and…"

"You blew the trip, Hattie. Good-bye." Bea hung up on her in mid-sentence. She wasn't about to get involved in that hassle.

Turning back to her closet, Bea resumed her clothing search. Within ten minutes she had settled on a royal blue designer pants suit with a matching shell. She was standing in front of the mirror admiring what she saw when the doorbell rang.

Bea's stomach jumped. Hattie had been correct. She really did like this man a lot. He actually made her feel weak in the knees. She hadn't felt this way in years, not since—

No! Not tonight. She was putting the past to rest. Squaring her shoulders, she whispered a quick prayer that the evening would go well, gathered her composure and prepared to meet her date.

When Bea opened the door she nearly fell to her knees. The man looked good enough to eat. Dressed in sharply creased brown pants and a beige knit shirt, his silver gray mane appeared to be freshly cut and the smile that he flashed at her was dazzling.

"Hello." His deep timbered greeting was nearly her undoing. "You look great."

Bea swallowed, hard. "Thank you."

"Are you ready to go?"

Nodding, she picked up her purse from a table in the entrance hall and took the hand that Joshua held out to her.

As the couple rode in the car in silence, Bea stole sly glances at Josh. He was handsome, intelligent and wealthy. Over the past few weeks during their many telephone conversations she had learned that he was also caring. It was almost like having Frank back again.

Bea started, jolted by the thought. She had to stop this. She had promised herself to put the past behind her. Comparing the two men was unfair. Thankfully, Josh's voice interrupted her musing.

"I did tell you how good you look tonight, didn't I?"

"Yes, you did. Thank you." Bea gave a soft smile. She wanted to add that he did too, but instead she turned and looked out of the window at the passing scenery.

Conversation between them was at a minimum as Joshua concentrated on getting them to their destination. As they continued driving, Bea began to notice the lights of the city fading. She frowned. Where were they? It was dark, really dark. There were no lights, or houses to be seen, nothing but trees along an isolated paved, two lane road. She had no clue where they were. She fought an uneasy feeling.

"Where are we going?"

Josh raised a brow. "Ah ha, so you're curious." He flashed that heart-stopping smile. "I didn't mean to be so mysterious about tonight's plans. I thought we'd do something different and I wanted to keep it a secret."

"So we're not going to dinner?"

"Oh, yes we are. Trust me; this place is one-of-a kind."

Bea was not a great one for surprises. "What do you mean by that?"

His only reply was a crooked smile and the silence in the car returned. Bea strained to see a familiar landmark in the darkness but could make out nothing. They pulled off the paved road they were on and turned onto a narrow graveled path. Except for the headlights, they were surrounded by pitch blackness. Her apprehension increased as she asked herself how much did she really know about this man? She turned to him.

"Look, Josh, I want to know where you're taking me and I want to know now."

"Don't get upset Bea." His voice was soothing. "I'm taking you to a special place and I think that you're going to like it."

A special place? That could mean a lot of things. Oh, Lord, don't let this man be a serial killer! The car came to a stop.

"Why are we stopping?" Bea demanded. "We're in the middle of nowhere!"

He grinned. "Don't worry. Didn't I tell you that you would be pleased? Just sit right here and I'll be back."

Bea objected. "Sit in the dark? By myself?"

"I'm locking the doors. I've got to check on something. I'll only be a minute." Visibly excited, Josh hopped out of the car and disappeared in the dark.

As soon as he was out of sight, Bea pulled her cell phone from her purse and dialed her son, Bryant. He was a police detective and would have the entire Indianapolis Police Department looking for her if it was needed. He answered.

"Bell here."

"Hello, Bryant, this is Mother." Bea spoke in a frantic whisper. "I'm sitting here in a car in the middle of nowhere. It's dark and Josh is gone." She blurted her message without a breath.

"Mother, what's going on?" Bryant sounded confused. "Are you hurt? And who is Josh?"

"I'm fine so far. I'm supposed to be on a date with Joshua Pierce—remember I mentioned him to you?"

"No you didn't!" His tone was stern.

"Oh well, I thought that I did. I can't remember. He drives an Aston Martin..."

"An Aston Martin!" Her son was a car buff.

"Yes, a white one and we're in it now. We started driving and I wasn't paying attention and then we stopped in the dark. I don't know where we are. Wait a minute—"

"Mother!" Bryant's confusion turned to alarm.

"He's coming back! I'm going to keep my cell phone on so you can listen. Trace the signal if you have to and send help." Quickly she slipped the cell phone into her jacket pocket just as Josh reached the car. He tapped on the window beckoning her to exit. Reluctantly, she opened the door.

"What kind of joke is this, Josh? I don't like this."

"It's not a joke, Bea." Taking her hand he helped her out of the car. "We're going to dinner just as I said." He put a protective arm around her waist and led her down a small dirt path bathed by the soft light of the moon.

"How far out of the city are we?" Bea inquired, speaking loudly enough with the hope that Bryant could hear her over the cell phone.

"Actually, we're just a little north of Fishers."

"North of Fishers," Bea repeated dutifully. "We're on a hill where there are no houses."

Josh nodded absently, thinking that she was speaking to him. "It is pretty isolated out here. The nearest house is about a quarter of a mile away."

Bea's eyes widened. A quarter of a mile to the nearest house! Oh, Lord they would never find her body.

She frantically contemplated how to feed Bryant more clues about her whereabouts, and then she saw light in the clearing ahead. As they drew closer she realized that this was the site of a house under construction. The foundation was laid and most of the framing completed. Strings of miniature lights surrounded the entire perimeter. In the center of the construction in one of the framed rooms a table had been placed. A white linen tablecloth covered it. Vases filled with bouquets of flowers of every variety ringed the room. Among the menagerie of blossoms were roses, mums, carnations, and daisies. Their fragrance permeated the air. The two place settings on the table were of fine china. The crystal goblets at each setting glistened like diamonds in the moonlight. Sterling silver candlesticks held tapered candles that flickered in the light breeze.

Bea was stunned. "What in the world?" She looked from the surreal scene before her back to Joshua. "How did you do this?"

Josh grinned, pleased by her response. He didn't answer her question. Instead, without a word he led her to one of the dining chairs and pulled it out with a flourish.

Bea tried to peer through the darkness beyond the dining area. "Where are we?"

Josh gave an eloquent sweep of his hand. "Welcome to my home."

She returned her attention to him. "What is this about?" Bea looked as confused as she sounded.

He clarified. "You may not recall but when I first met you I said that I was building a house. This is it. Since I'm moving my headquarters to Indy, I can't continue living in an apartment." He seated Bea in the chair and whispered in her ear. "Who knows, this house may become a real home someday."

Still dazed by the unexpected turn of events, she spotted a silver serving cart. It was laden with covered trays.

"Where did all of this come from? We're in the middle of nowhere."

"For the right price you can get a caterer to deliver anywhere. I'm just glad that they managed to find the place." Josh rubbed his hands together eagerly. "We can eat right away if you'd like, or we can go dancing."

Bea raised a brow. "Dancing? Where would we go dancing? Are we going to leave all of this out here?" She gestured around.

"Who said anything about leaving?" Going to the serving cart, he reached beneath it to the last shelf and turned on a portable CD player. Soft music drifted into the star filled night. Returning to Bea, he held out his hand.

"May I?"

In a daze, she rose from her chair and floated into his arms. His hold was firm and confident. The beat of his heart was strong and steady, and the scent of his cologne was intoxicating. Somehow Bea managed to keep step as they glided along the cement floor in perfect sync with the music and with each other. When the final notes of the sexy saxophone drifted into the surrounding woods they continued swaying to music that only they could hear.

Gradually they came to a stop. Entranced, Bea chanced a look up at Joshua. His eyes were waiting. For a second they stood silently, lost in each other's gaze.

Josh broke the spell with a seductive whisper. "I could get used to this."

"Get used to what?"

"The way you feel in my arms."

Bea gulped. She didn't know what to say.

Tilting Bea's chin, he looked into her eyes. "I'll be in Vegas completing some business the same time you'll be there."

"W…will you?" Bea's mouth went dry.

"And I plan on you being in my arms like this while you're there."

Joshua inclined his head and Bea shivered in anticipation certain that she would die on the spot. If so, she would die happy. She had no doubt about that, and when his lips touched hers she knew that to be true. They were both so lost in the moment that for a second neither of them heard the faint noise coming from her jacket pocket.

"Mother?" It was Bryant's muffled voice. Her phone was still on.

Breaking the kiss, Josh nibbled at the corner of her mouth. "What was that?"

Bea nibbled back. "My cell phone."

Groping for the intruding contraption, she answered its call. "I'll see you later, dear." She turned it off and placed it back in her jacket pocket.

"Who was that?" His interest appeared mild as he worked his way leisurely down her neck. Bea shivered.

"My son—uh, what's his name?"

Josh's hot breath blazed a flaming path across her breast. "Should I be concerned?"

Bea moaned. "Absolutely not."

She had been as sure about that as she was that she would see him again. God hadn't dangled the hope for happiness with another man before her without delivering. So the panic that Hattie was displaying about the possibility of crashing annoyed her because Bea planned on landing in Vegas in one piece.

****

During the weeks before the trip, Hattie's effort to talk Miss Fanny into giving up the ticket to Las Vegas had intensified. She tried appealing to the older woman's sense of fairness by pointing out to her that she only got the ticket by default. After all, Connie was her friend and had offered the ticket to her first.

Miss Fanny had laughed and told her, "Too bad."

When that didn't work, Hattie tried to elicit her sympathy by informing her about how high the price of a round trip ticket would be at such short notice if she had to purchase one.

"You know that it's difficult to afford such an expense on Leon's pension," she told her mother-in-law.

Miss Fanny didn't bend. Instead, she reminded Hattie of her thriving new business that should be supplementing her already generous pension quite nicely. She then advised her to purchase one of the cheap Las Vegas packages that were constantly being offered and to leave her alone.

Once again Hattie appealed to Bea—who was so caught up with that Joshua fellow that she could hardly think straight. She asked her to speak to the selfish old woman for her, but her plea continued to fall on deaf ears as her best friend in the world, the woman who served as her maid of honor at her wedding and as the godmother to her eldest child, refused to intervene. As a matter of fact she sided with Miss Fanny. Hattie felt as though she didn't have a soul left who she could turn too but Jesus, so she did just that. She prayed that he would soften Miss Fanny's hardened heart, but He must have been busy with war and pestilence because as the date for the trip drew closer it looked as though Hattie would have to purchase a very expensive airplane ticket if she wanted to take the trip with them. And then Connie called.

"Hattie, I heard from Miss Fanny that you've been trying to—and this is her word, not mine—'cheat' her out of her ticket to Las Vegas.

"Cheat her!" Hattie was insulted. "Nobody is trying to cheat her! That was my ticket in the first place…"

"Which you said you didn't want," Connie reminded her. "But don't worry; David has come to the rescue."

"David? David who?"

Connie gave a prolonged sigh. "My friend, David. The one who you met at the auction"

"Oh, him." Hattie wondered how she was expected to keep up with Connie's men. Between her and Bea they were dropping from the sky like rain drops.

"Yes, him," Connie continued. "I gave him one of the tickets to Vegas, but when he heard about your change of mind, he generously offered to give you his ticket. He's buying another one."

"Do Jesus!" Hattie couldn't believe her luck. "Well you tell Daniel…"

"David."

"You tell David that he doesn't have to do that."

"Okay, I will," Connie agreed eagerly. It was her opinion that he was being too generous anyway.

"But, that I accept his offer and I can't thank him enough." Hattie wasn't about to let this opportunity slip away

When they disconnected, Hattie let out a whoop that sent Miss Fanny scurrying from her room in alarm. She found her daughter-in-law prancing around the living room doing a happy dance.

"What in the world is wrong with you?"

"For your information I'm going to Las Vegas too," Hattie sniffed smugly. "It turned out that I didn't need your old ticket."

"Well good for you," Miss Fanny didn't appear to be too surprised. "Who got you the ticket, the reverend?"

"You have got to be kidding!" Hattie's balloon deflated. "You know good and well that he's in Las Vegas preparing for the convention. Anyway, I wouldn't take a gift like that from a man..." She hesitated since that was exactly what she had done, so she added, "that I know well."

"Uh huh." Miss Fanny turned and headed back to her room. "So I guess we're both going to Sin City."

"I guess so." Hattie couldn't contain her glee.

"But for different reasons," Miss Fanny tossed over her shoulder.

"Right again. You're going to sin and I'm going to the annual church convention for the purpose of serving my Jesus."

"Yeah," Miss Fanny grunted. "And when you get there I hope you can live with that lie." She disappeared down the hall.

Hattie called after her. "I don't care what you think; the bottom line is the Spirit is sending me to Las Vegas."

It was that half truth that had placed Hattie on this airplane flight. She had let lust lead her to Sin City, and the Lord had sent her warning signs that he wasn't pleased. Foolishly, she had ignored them all.

CHAPTER 7

As far as Hattie was concerned, the warning signs had started when they arrived at the airport. Bea and Connie had vowed that if they both lived to be a hundred years old, they would never go on a trip with Hattie and Miss Fanny again. The two women sat huddled in the airport terminal glaring at Hattie and her mother-in-law with looks of murderous intent.

"I have never been so embarrassed in my life," Bea whispered to Connie. Her eyes shifted briefly to David to make sure that he was out of ear shot as he headed for a nearby coffee shop. Her eyes went back to the subjects at hand. "Look at them sitting over there looking as innocent as lambs. It was bad enough when Hattie raised a fuss about taking off her shoes at the gate and then tried to take off her knee-highs too, but when Miss Fanny reached into her bra to get her "bosom money…"

"And she had to take that old handkerchief stuffed with coins out of her bra..." Connie had to admit that the memory amused her.

"I nearly died," Bea continued, not amused at all by the incident.

"I told David to walk fast so people wouldn't think that they were with us." Connie was still angry about how Hattie had shouted her name across the terminal to have them wait for her. She sounded like some farmer calling his pigs.

"We should have let the security guards haul both of them away when they tried to smuggle contraband aboard," Bea huffed. "I'm surprised that the Airport Authority hasn't called Homeland Security."

"Don't speak too soon," Connie warned. "We still haven't boarded the plane."

Across the aisle from Bea and Connie sat a grumbling Hattie, who was not happy with her friends at all.

"Those two hussies should have told us that we couldn't pack food to take with us on a plane," Hattie pouted as she returned their pointed glares. "That was twenty dollars worth of ham and chicken sandwiches those people took from us."

"I wonder if we can get reimbursed." Miss Fanny couldn't believe the injustice of it all. "Shoot, you can bring food on the bus and train! I don't know what's wrong with these people."

She was still mad about having to reveal her secret stash. If those security perverts hadn't made her go through that body scan no one would have known about her money. She had been forced to remove it from her bra. Now that people knew where she kept her mad money she was fair game for every crook and thug in the airport.

Miss Fanny tightened her hold on her good purse and looked as mean as possible. At least the pickpockets and purse snatchers would know that just because she was older she wasn't easy prey. She'd give them a fight for her money.

"I like the train better anyway," Hattie stated firmly. "Not only can you bring your own food, but there's room to walk around and stretch. We should have taken a train to Las Vegas."

Miss Fanny huffed. "I'd rather be on solid ground than up there in God's sky."

"Amen to that." Hattie couldn't have said it better.

This seemed like the first time that she and Miss Fanny had actually found something on which they agreed. Neither had ever flown before and both were admittedly nervous about it, not that they were getting any sympathy from Bea and Connie. But, each woman had her own reasons for wanting to go to Vegas and those reasons overshadowed their fears.

"All we can do is pray and put ourselves in the Lord's hand." Hattie bowed her head and joined hands with Miss Fanny as they each prayed silently.

"At least they're not jumping up and down and doing a holy dance," Connie said to Bea as she watched the two women sitting across from them praying.

"They're not on the airplane yet," Bea warned. "When it takes off we'd better brace ourselves for anything."

Bea's words proved prophetic when the five of them boarded the airplane. Miss Fanny started her performance before the plane took off.

Bea, Connie and David sat together in the row across from Hattie and Miss Fanny. Sitting in the aisle seat across from the older woman and her daughter-in-law, David was more sympathetic to the two novice flyers. He helped Hattie and Miss Fanny put their carryon luggage in the overhead compartment and showed them where the oxygen and overhead lights were located.

Miss Fanny's seat was by the window, but she didn't want to sit there so that she could see "how far they could fall from the sky". So it was David who negotiated a seat exchange with the man in the aisle seat who sat next to the ladies. Hattie was content with her middle seat and had no complaints. She turned to the middle aged stranger who had been kind enough to exchange seats with her mother-in-law.

"I want to thank you for your kindness Mr.—" She paused, awaiting an introduction.

"Smith, Larry Smith." The man acknowledged her with a nod. It was obvious that he wasn't interested in continuing the conversation as he turned to look out of the window. It was a cue that Hattie appeared to miss.

"Mr. Smith," she continued, "This is my mother-in-law's first time on an airplane. Mine too."

The man turned, nodded again, and then turned back to the window. Hattie ignored that cue as well.

"Do you know Jesus, Mr. Smith?"

The question seemed to catch the man off guard as he turned to study Hattie for a moment. "Not personally. Is he a neighbor of yours?"

Hattie ignored the sarcasm. Here was a soul that might need salvation, so she zeroed in on a possible opportunity.

"He's my neighbor, my colleague and my friend," she informed him earnestly. "I woke up with him on my mind this morning and I go to bed with his name on my lips every night."

Overhearing the conversation, Miss Fanny added an "Amen."

Amused, Mr. Smith's lip curled upward. "Well I'm glad that you're so intimate with the man. I'm afraid that I'm not that close to him. As a matter of fact, I'm not close at all. I don't believe in Jesus or God. You see I'm an atheist."

That was the second sign, one that Hattie could not ignore. She was sitting next to a godless man. Flabbergasted, she and Miss Fanny stared at him as if he had two heads. Miss Fanny elbowed Hattie and whispered loudly.

"Did he say that he didn't believe in Jesus or God?"

Stunned into silence, Hattie could only nod her head. She had never met anybody in her life who didn't believe in her Lord and Savior. Was he serious? She had to ask.

"Are you kidding?"

"No" was all that he could utter before they prepared for takeoff. The flight attendant's safety demonstration caught Hattie and Miss Fanny's attention. After that they both studied the seating card intently, counting the number of seats they would have to navigate to get them to the plane's exit.

"Lord, I sure hope we don't go down over water," Hattie lamented. "Neither one of us can swim."

"And I don't believe for a minute that no seat cushion is gonna float," sniffed Miss Fanny. "A seat cushion is a seat cushion. It ain't no boat. What kind of fools do they take us for?"

Settling in for takeoff, Bea searched through her purse and found the package of gum that she had been looking for. She withdrew two pieces and nudged Connie.

"Ask David to pass these to Hattie and Miss Fanny and tell them to chew it when we take off so that their ears won't pop."

Connie took the gum. "Good idea. That's all we need is for those two to start running up and down the aisle talking about how they're going deaf."

Giving the gum to David, she passed on Bea's instructions. Both women complied and chewed the gum, but when the plane started to climb upward pleas of "Lord Have Mercy" and "Do Jesus" drifted across the aisle to Bea and Connie.

Hattie and Miss Fanny clenched each other's hands desperate for some sort of security. As the sound of the airplane's engines roared in their ears, they bowed their heads in prayer begging silently for deliverance if the plane went down. Neither woman stopped praying or opened her eyes until the flight leveled off in the sky.

Miss Fanny was the first one to open her eyes—at least one of them. She did so slowly and looked around. The airplane was quiet and it was still in the air. Nobody was panicking so she figured that everything must be all right. Opening the other eye, she elbowed Hattie.

"What?" Hattie's eyes were still closed and her tone was harsh. She was anxious to get back to prayer. As long as she was God knows how high up in the sky it was needed.

Miss Fanny chose to ignore her attitude. "You can open your eyes. Everything is okay."

Cautiously, Hattie opened one eye and then the other. Everything appeared to be fine. Nobody was in the aisle but the flight attendant and she looked calm. Relaxing, Hattie released Miss Fanny's hand and took a big breath.

"Are you two ladies all right over there?" David inquired.

"We're fine," Hattie reassured him, impressed with his genuine concern. He seemed to be such a nice man. It made her wonder why Connie hadn't introduced him sooner.

"Thank you for asking," Miss Fanny smiled at him graciously. "Unlike the people sitting next to you who shall remain nameless, you've got a heart." She rolled her eyes at Hattie's friends.

The flight continued smoothly for a while as Hattie and Miss Fanny, still on edge, sat observing everything and everyone around them. When the seat belt sign flashed clear for them to unbuckle, both ladies declined the request.

"If I'm going down," Miss Fanny noted, "I want to be found in one piece strapped to my seat. They won't be finding pieces of me scattered all over the place."

"That's right." Hattie shook her head vigorously. "When I see my Savior I want him to recognize me."

She turned to her dozing seat mate and continued their previous conversation. "So you say that you don't know Jesus."

Larry Smith started awake. The look on his face when he turned to Hattie made it clear that her inquiry was unwelcomed. Staring at her blankly, he said nothing, but if he wasn't talking Hattie certainly was. This was one godless soul who needed to hear the Word.

She was well on her way to delivering one of her sermons when the man held up his hand to stop her flow of words. He pulled no punches.

"Listen Lady, I told you that I'm an atheist, so I don't want to hear it. I paid good money for this seat and I mean to fly in peace." With that he whipped out an Ipod, jammed the earphones on, leaned back against the head rest and closed his eyes. He had effectively closed Hattie out of his consciousness.

"Well!" She had never been so insulted in her life.

Having witnessed the entire episode, Miss Fanny offered a word of comfort to her daughter-in-law. "Don't worry." She patted her hand. "He's godless. He'll be going to hell soon anyway."

The travelers were a few hours into their flight when the pilot announced over the intercom that they were flying over the Grand Canyon. Excited, Bea, Connie and David strained to see one of the world's natural wonders. Not wanting Hattie and Miss Fanny to miss the spectacular sight, Connie leaned over David and urged the two women to look out the window.

Miss Fanny wasn't impressed. "If you've seen one hole in the ground you've seen them all." She tightened her hold on her purse.

Looking up from reading her Bible Hattie declined the offer. "No thank you. I'm fine."

At that moment, as she tried to return to her reading, the airplane seemed to drop several feet. That had been the third sign. Hattie sat straight up in her seat.

"Lord, have mercy!" She looked at Miss Fanny. Both women were wide-eyed.

"What was that?" Miss Fanny reached up and buzzed for assistance.

The young, blond flight attendant seemed reluctant when she answered the call. "May I help you—again?"

"What was that shaking?" Miss Fanny asked with concern.

"It's nothing to worry about, just a little turbulence."

"Terrorist?" Hattie's head jerked up. "Did you say terrorist?" The fear in her voice drifted across several aisles, catching the attention of other passengers. Several of them leaned into the aisle to see what was happening.

The aggravated flight attendant gave a frustrated sigh as she addressed the other passengers. "That was just a little turbulence, folks. Everything is fine." She turned back to Miss Fanny.

"Ma'am since getting on this flight, you have insulted the captain…"

"What do you mean insulted? He don't look like he's old enough to fly a plane…"

"You have called the attendants back here at least five times, asking about arrival times."

"I wanted to know what time this contraption is landing. So sue me!"

"You got stuck in the bathroom twice…"

"Who on earth can use them tiny bathrooms? It ain't nothing but a flying outhouse…"

"Your daughter…"

"She's my daughter-in-law."

"Has complained about us serving alcohol…"

"The devil's brew!" It was Hattie's turn to jump into the dispute.

"And don't forget how that old one over there," the passenger in the seat in front of them pointed to Miss Fanny, "threatened to throw my poor little boy off the plane if he didn't stop running up and down the aisle."

"Sho' 'nough," Miss Fanny held her head up proudly. "Your kid is a brat!"

A second attendant hurried up the aisle to assess the situation. "Is there a problem here?" she asked her harried co-worker. She looked concerned until she noticed the source of the brewing disturbance.

"Oh, you two." She shifted her attention back to the attendant. "What's the problem this time?"

Larry Smith spoke up. "The problem is that I'm not flying on your airline again as long as I live! I'm demanding my money back for this flight and I'll tell you why! First, I was asked by these two women to change my seat, and for my kindness what did I get? Harassed! I've been accused of being an alcoholic because I ordered a drink. I can't get any sleep. I can't listen to my music and I nearly had a heart attack when that one said that there were terrorists on the plane." He pointed to Hattie.

The older attendant looked at the other one in alarm and whispered, "Terrorists? What terrorists?"

"I'll explain it to you later." The young woman returned her attention to the two passengers. "Listen ladies, we have been more than patient with you. Any more disturbances and we'll have to call airport security to meet you at the terminal."

Miss Fanny would not be intimidated, "Well you can just…" The airplane lurched violently, stopping her words.

It was then that Hattie screamed, "We're going down!"

Her words put the airplane in turmoil as passengers panicked. The stewardesses were scurrying around frantically trying to calm people down. In her own state of alarm, Hattie audibly called on the Lord with a loud prayer mode.

"Sweet Jesus, please don't let this plane go down. If you get us through this trial of fire I promise that I will follow a righteous path in that city of sin and see that Thy will be done."

That was the promise that Hattie Collier made to her Lord and Master, and she meant to keep her word.

CHAPTER 8

On their arrival at their Las Vegas hotel, Connie Palmer and Bea Bell marched across the lobby like soldiers and both were as mad as hell. Small beads of perspiration formed over Connie's taunt lips. Bea's jaw muscles twitched uncontrollably. Following a short distance behind was a contrite Hattie and a defiant Miss Fanny.

"It was humiliating enough before we got on the plane," Connie growled at Bea, "but when Hattie yelled that we were crashing…" Connie's mouth clamped shut as all-consuming anger took hold again.

"Thank goodness that it didn't take the flight attendants long to get people calmed down. It was when we were met by airport security that I wanted to beat Hattie and Miss Fanny into the ground. That weird little security person looked like she wanted to do a strip search on us all." Bea shuddered at the memory. Thank God they had just patted them down.

"All I know is that if I never take a trip with Hattie and Miss Fanny again, it will be too soon." This last comment was thrown over Connie's shoulder loud enough for the two culprits to hear.

Hattie wasn't going to take the criticism lying down. "Well, how was I supposed to know that the stewardess said the word turbulence? I thought she said terrorist! I never heard of turbulence before! The way that plane was bumping and dipping, I thought that we'd hit a mountain or something. I could have sworn I was going home to my Jesus."

"If you don't tread real lightly, that may be arranged," Connie barked.

Hattie was riled. "I don't know why you're complaining. At least security gave you back all of your possessions. After they searched my things, one of my Bibles was missing. I hope the heathen that took it has the good sense to read it."

"Oh stop sniveling," snapped Miss Fanny. "If it hadn't been for me you three fools could be rotting in prison. I was the one who reasoned with security and let them know that we weren't dangerous."

"Reasoned?" Connie barked. "You went on and on about your heart and how it might give out at any moment. You played the age card beautifully, but I don't call that reasoning."

"For someone so sick you sure had a miraculous recovery," Bea added.

The feuding quartet caught up with David, who had happily gone ahead of the women to check in at the hotel desk.

"I've got the rooms." He held up two key cards. "These are for you three ladies," he said to Bea, Hattie and Miss Fanny.

Bea glowered at him. "You've got to be kidding! If you think that I'm going to stay in a room with these two psychos you've got another think coming!"

Ignoring Bea, Miss Fanny looked puzzled as she glanced at the room keys. "Why are the three of us together? I thought Bea and Connie were in the same room?"

"David and I are staying together." Connie gave the older woman a smug smile.

Hattie's mouth dropped open. "How long must I pray for you, Connie, before you stop sinning? Now you gonna take this good man to hell with you?"

Those words started a brand new round of sparing as Connie took a step toward Hattie and informed her that she was a grown woman and that she would do what she dammed well pleased. The fight was ready for round two when it was suddenly stopped by a squeal of delight from Bea. Everyone looked in her direction and then their eyes followed her gaze. Striding toward them was a smiling Joshua Pierce. An excited Bea rushed into his embrace.

"Surprise!" He kissed her warmly.

"What are you doing here?" Bea was beaming. The mere sight of him had instantly soothed her spirit.

He held her in his loose embrace. "Remember when I told you that I would be in Las Vegas the same time you would be here? I'm shutting down my office. The timing was perfect."

"I'm so glad to see you." Bea couldn't wipe the grin off of her face. "Where are you staying?"

"Right here at this hotel. I didn't want to be too far away from you."

Bea blushed. Miss Fanny wasn't impressed.

"Yeah, yeah. If y'all don't mind, I've had a very tiring trip and I'd like to get to the room." She hugged her purse to her chest and looked at the group expectantly. Bea glowered at her, as did Connie.

Josh noticed the awkwardness between the four women. He turned to Bea, "What's wrong?"

Over her head he saw David moving his hand in a 'cut' motion across his throat signaling him not to ask the question. It was too late. The floodgates were opened and everyone tried to explain at once.

"Hattie scared the hell out of everybody by yelling that the plane was crashing!" Bea bellowed.

"Well it sure felt like it was!" Hattie huffed.

"The airline threatened to have security haul us away when we were at the terminal," Connie added.

Bea's ire flared again. "Security did haul us away."

"Aw, ya'll just big cry babies," Miss Fanny dismissed both of them.

"Ladies, please!" David intervened. "Can we all just get along?" He had been patient with the four of them so far, but now he was getting frustrated. He turned to Josh. "Man, we had quite a time getting here and I think that everyone needs to settle down and cool off."

Once again he offered the keys to Bea. Once again she ignored them.

"I told you, I'm getting my own room. I'm not staying with those two." Walking to the check in desk she requested a room.

The desk clerk, who had been discretely listening to the squabble, looked at her with concern. "I'm sorry but we are completely booked."

Bea looked disappointed, but not defeated. "Then I guess I'll have to find someplace else to stay. There are plenty of hotels in Las Vegas. Josh will you help me with my bags?"

"Bea, you don't have a reservation any place else," Connie stated anxiously. "And you don't know this town. Anything could happen."

"Then it looks like you're stuck with us," Hattie grunted triumphantly.

For a second Bea appeared hesitant. Then she looked Hattie squarely in the eye. "I'm staying with Josh."

"What?" Josh was so shocked that he dropped her bags.

"I'm staying with you," Bea stated again flatly.

Josh wasn't sure how to respond. "W-w-well, I do have a suite and there is plenty of room."

"Are you sure?" Connie was as surprised as everyone else.

As far as Miss Fanny was concerned the matter was settled. "She's grown. I'm ready to get to my room."

Hattie was not convinced. "She's not serious. She's just mad at me and showing off."

Everyone looked at Bea expectantly. She turned to Josh. "What floor are you on?"

He answered quietly, "I'm in a penthouse suite."

Picking up one of her bags, Bea turned toward the elevators and without another word walked away. Josh caught her elbow and steered her in the opposite direction.

"The private elevators are this way."

Connie raised an eyebrow but said nothing. Hattie gasped and Miss Fanny summed up that announcement with a "Humph! At least she'll be sinning in style. "

****

After settling in their room, an exhausted Connie laid on the bed as David gently massaged her back. She let out a luxurious sigh.

"Are you calming down?" He worked his way down her lower back,

As an answer, Connie patted the bed, inviting him to lie down beside her. He complied, putting an arm around her and drawing her close. She snuggled up to him with her mind still on today's fiasco.

"I could have killed those two. I've never been so humiliated in my life. I was scared to death."

David chuckled. "I have to admit that the thought of getting arrested on some Federal charge didn't make me happy. I wasn't looking forward to sitting out the next six months in prison. But I'll say one thing, being around you and your friends is definitely not boring."

Connie had to agree, but she also had to admit that some of Hattie and Miss Fanny's antics were funny. As she thought about it she tried to hold a giggle, but before long both she and David were laughing so hard that they could barely breathe. He wrapped an arm around Connie as she wiped tears of mirth from her eyes.

"Do you feel better?" David asked. "You're much more beautiful when you laugh."

She flashed him a fond smile. "I have to say that being mortified and manhandled by strangers doesn't seem that funny."

David wiggled his eyebrows. "Would you feel better if you were manhandled by someone you knew?"

"Try it and I'll call the cops," teased Connie.

He flipped her on her back and breathed into her ear. "Oh, you'll be calling somebody all right, all night long"

His mouth covered hers, as he kissed her hungrily and proceeded to keep his word.

****

Bea was aware of Joshua studying her as she walked around his luxurious suite. He sat in the sitting room as she took in the plush carpet and the expensive furnishings. There was a wet bar in the living room and an electric fireplace separating it from the dining area, although Bea didn't quite understand the need for a fireplace in this desert heat.

The master bedroom suite was located in the loft at the top of a winding staircase. It was dominated by a round, king-sized bed that she hurried pass nervously. In the adjoining bathroom was a Jacuzzi that could accommodate two people quite comfortably, but she wasn't sure that was going to happen.

Bea knew that it had been difficult for Josh to contain his surprise or his pleasure when she decided to stay with him. But as she gave an account of their trip to Las Vegas, it must have became obvious to him that she had not been in her right mind when she made that sudden decision. Hattie and Miss Fanny could drive anybody crazy.

"I expected this trip to be fun," Bea told him. The tour had ended and she was sitting beside him in the living room on a very comfortable sofa. "I thought that it would be something different from anything I've done in a while, but this is too much. It's definitely been different. But fun? I don't think so"

"Bea."

"Yes?" Her name on Josh's lips never ceased to make her knees quake.

He took her hand in his. "You came on this trip to have a good time and I'm going to make it my personal business to see that you do." He kissed the back of her hand, and then rising from the sofa he started unbuttoning his shirt as he walked across the room toward the stairs.

Bea gasped. "What are you doing?"

Josh turned and gave her a puzzled look. "I'm not going out on the town like this. I've got to change my shirt." He started up the stairs and then suddenly halted his steps as understanding dawned. He turned back to Bea. "Look, I know your decision to stay with me was made on a whim, so I don't want you to get the wrong idea. It's not like we planned your being here…"

"I know."

"So I don't want you to think that I'm going to pressure you into doing anything."

"O-Oh, I wasn't thinking anything like that," Bea lied.

"The master bedroom is yours. I'll take the smaller bedroom down here."

"Uh, okay. But go ahead and change. If you'll excuse me, I'll just go to the bathroom down here and freshen up." Bea beat a hasty retreat and closed the bathroom door firmly behind her. Breathing a sigh of relief, she peered in the wall length mirror hanging over the marble vanity. She was sweating like a pig in heat. It was time to have a serious talk with herself. She had to get a grip.

Girl, don't start acting like a schoolgirl. Yes, the man is gorgeous, but Lord have mercy, don't be a fool!

With her anger at Hattie now temporarily forgotten, Bea began to curse her impulsive decision to stay with Josh. Was she really going to sleep here tonight with just a staircase between them? Would they be able to contain themselves and stay away from each other? Or perhaps a better question might be could she contain herself?

****

Fourteen floors down, Hattie and Miss Fanny entered their suite. It was quite nice, with two bedrooms and a sitting room. Miss Fanny and Hattie turned into the closest bedroom, which the older woman claimed as her own. With a weary sigh, Miss Fanny sat down on one of the beds and surveyed her surroundings. She noted the plush carpeting, the gold brocade bedspreads on the two queen-sized beds, the matching wingback chairs, and the thirty-two inch television hanging on the wall. Her eyes came to rest on her daughter-in-law who sat dejectedly in one of the chairs looking out the window.

"Hattie Mae Collier, stop sitting there looking like you've been sucking on a lemon. We came here to enjoy ourselves, not to mope and complain."

"It's easy for you to say. Your friends aren't mad at you. They'd rather live in sin than sleep in the same room as me.

"Oh, get over it. You can't help it if you got good lungs and scared the living daylights out of those people on the plane."

Hattie wasn't sure that Miss Fanny was being sympathetic. "Well I'm still mad at those attendants for calling security on us. I thank God that they didn't arrest us. What if we'd been put in jail and it got back to the church?"

Miss Fanny wasn't fooled. "You mean what if it got back to your precious reverend."

Hattie's cheeks turned hot. "I'll thank you to keep Reverend Trees out of this."

"All right then." Miss Fanny pushed herself off the bed and picked up her purse. She walked to the door and flung it open. "I'm outta here."

"And where do you think you're going?" Hattie demanded.

"Not that it's any of your business, but they call this place Sin City and I'm going to find out why."

The door slammed behind her leaving Hattie feeling even more forlorn. What in the world was happening? First, she and her life-long friends were fighting and then Connie stopped pretending to be a Jezebel and just came right out with it. Now Bea, who was already teetering on the brink, just completely gave in to sin. Last but not least Miss Fanny was going off to find corruption. What would her husband, Leon, say if he was here to witness his mother's actions?

"Lord, I need a word from you," Hattie muttered aloud.

She started a frantic search for her Bible and then remembered that her large one had been confiscated by security, but she wasn't going to be defeated. She had heard that every hotel room had a Bible. Going to one of the bedside tables she pulled the drawer open. An ink pen and a small notepad embossed with the hotel's name were the only items inside. She walked around the bed to the other table, but found only a guide to the points of interest in Las Vegas. There was no Bible! Either someone must have stolen it, or worse, it was never there. Another sign! The city of Las Vegas was taunting her—daring her, challenging her to accept its evil ways; but she was here and she was going to take a stand for righteousness wherever she saw sin.

CHAPTER 9

Hattie felt that she had been abandoned. She had been tossed aside like an old shoe. She was all but alone in Las Vegas with nowhere to turn. This place was the devil's playground and he was working overtime on the people that she loved. Both Bea and Connie were knee deep in the sin of the flesh, shacking up with men. As for Miss Fanny, she wasn't sure where she was. The old lady had been AWOL since she left the room that morning, so Hattie had ventured downstairs to check out the hotel.

Lord have mercy, she had never seen so much of Satan's work in one place in all of her life. She had gone to one of the hotel's bathrooms and a slot machine was in there. Whoever heard of such a thing?

Hattie was thinking about marching through that glitzy lobby just like Jesus, running the sinners out into the street. All of this was a bit too much for her. She had to get out of here so that she could be among Christians. The annual church convention hadn't started but there was the Exposition associated with it. Vendors from all over the country had brought their Christian wares to sell. That would be a good place to visit. Who knew, maybe she might bump into Reverend Trees.

He had informed her that part of his responsibility in assisting with the convention was helping to organize the exhibit booths. If she saw him there, she could surprise him. She hadn't told him that she was coming to town. Since there seemed to be no one in her life at the moment that cared whether she lived or died, she might as well go shopping!

Having made up her mind, Hattie tucked her purse tightly under her arm and made her way through the casino, looking neither left nor right as she headed toward the lobby. Just before reaching her destination, out of the corner of her eye she spotted Miss Fanny. Her mother-in-law was seated at a slot machine seemingly mesmerized by the contraption. The woman was so absorbed by what she was doing that at first she didn't notice her daughter-in-law. Hattie tapped her on the shoulder and Miss Fanny barely looked up.

"What?" She hit a button and pictures and symbols began to spin.

"I have been worried to death. Where have you been?

"Down here gambling." She gleefully pulled the slot machine arm.

"Well thanks a lot for letting me know! If you remember we came here for a religious convention and you're sitting here setting a horrible Christian example."

"An example for who? I don't know nobody here. Besides, I said I might go to the convention. You're the one using that excuse for being here." Miss Fanny didn't break stride as she continued to minister to the one-armed bandit.

Hattie exhaled her frustration. "In case you might be interested, I'm going to the convention hall and shop at the Expo they've set up there."

Absently, Miss Fanny waved her away and an agitated Hattie walked out of the hotel into the desert heat where she hailed a cab. That was the last time she would worry about that old broad!

The ride through the streets of Las Vegas proved to be a revelation. Apparently there was more sin here than she first thought. Mistakenly she had assumed that the gambling casinos and the hoochie-coochie joints that she had seen near her hotel was the extent of the vice in this city.

Hattie had never paid any attention to news about Las Vegas. As a Christian woman, why would it interest her? She did know that there was a strip of hotels in the town where all of the vice took place. She thought that's where their hotel was located, but as the cab weaved through the streets she began to realize how wrong she had been. Sin was everywhere in this city! Every time that she looked up there it was staring her in the face.

She counted one church in a ten block radius—at least the place might have been a church, it had a cross on top of it. But there were chapels all over the place, so many that she lost count. The cab driver told her that he doubted that they held church services in them because they were strictly for people to get married. Hattie took solace in the thought that at least marriage was still sacred in this town. Still, there were a lot of souls to be saved in Las Vegas—quick and in a hurry.

****

Connie loved Las Vegas. This was her kind of town. There was always something going on, nonstop action 24 hours a day.

It was here that she had met David at a realtor's convention. They had talked extensively during the workshop sessions, and during a break in the meetings Connie had decided to try her hand at the slot machines. To her great surprise she had looked up from one of them and found herself sitting next to David. Neither had any luck winning so on a whim they switched seats and they both won! That evening they went to a dinner show together to celebrate and they had been together ever since.

Visiting Las Vegas was proving to be even more fun this time, especially since it was on someone else's dime. Her prize package not only included hotel and airfare, but tickets to some of the hottest shows in town. A limousine was at their disposal and there were free meals for her three guests and herself. Of course there turned out to be six of them rather than four, but it was working out fine.

She had distributed the tickets and meal coupons prior to their trip so Hattie and Miss Fanny could go dine whenever they wished. She and Bea used the remaining coupons and David and Josh paid for their own meals. Between the show tickets and limo, she and Bea were having the time of their lives. They had two handsome escorts and they were living the Las Vegas experience big time.

Connie and Bea hadn't been on a double date together since their husbands were alive. It was especially fun since Joshua knew the city so well. He and David had hit it off from the moment they met and the two couples complemented each other very well. Since their arrival 24 short hours ago they had gambled nonstop, and between casinos they had gone to a revue show. This evening the two couples had front row seats to see one of the nation's hottest comedy acts. Every moment was chocked full of activity.

As Connie strolled through the hotel casino looking for just the right slot machine on which to play, she was thinking about the show this evening. David was in their room resting, but she had been too antsy. She was in Vegas and she wanted to enjoy every single moment.

Sipping a drink, Connie was taking in the surrounding sights and sounds when a familiar voice halted her footsteps.

"All right! That's what I'm talking about!"

Connie zeroed in on the direction from which the joyous words had come and found its source—Miss Fanny. She sat perched on a stool pumping her fist in the air in triumph. The colorful blinking lights and happy music coming from her slot machine indicated that she was a winner. Connie hurried over to her.

"Miss Fanny, how much did you win?" She asked, excited for her.

The older woman didn't look up. She pointed to the chart on the top of the machine as she continued to watch the symbols spin. "I've won three bucks so far." The machine kept spinning.

Connie looked confused. "Is that all?"

Miss Fanny turned to look at her. "Hey! I'm happy with it. This place is great! I didn't have to spend none of my money. If you're a first time gambler the hotel will give you a $5.00 credit on that card that you put into the machine." She nodded toward the object in question. "Five dollars free money."

She pulled the handle. The machine let her know that she had won again.

"Forty dollars! Have mercy! This is the deal of the century."

Her eyes sparkled with excitement as she cashed out. She waved the credit ticket in the air triumphantly as she turned to Connie. "I figure if every hotel in Vegas does this $5.00 credit thing I don't have to spend a dime while I'm here. I'm gonna hit every one of them around here and then go to the Strip and hit that from beginning to end." Miss Fanny slid from her seat.

"This place is a gold mine!"

"I never thought of it quite that way." Connie had to admit that she was impressed by her ingenuity. "Have you seen Hattie? Is she down here with you?"

"Are you kidding? She's at the convention I guess. As for me I'm going to go get my money and then play the machines at another hotel." She started down the aisle.

"Are you going to the convention?" Connie called after her above the din.

"Maybe later," Miss Fanny tossed over her shoulder.

As Connie watched her walk away, she got the impression that the only thing that could lure Miss Fanny to the annual church convention would be if they had slot machines there.

CHAPTER 10

On Hattie's first full day in Las Vegas her ride to the convention site was full of surprises. When her cab stopped at a light a young man came up to her window and tried to give her some kind of card with a picture of a naked woman on it. He was trying to convince her to come to some sort of nudie show. She rebuked him in the name of Jesus.

Hattie asked the taxi driver about such goings on and he shrugged as if it was an everyday occurrence. He told her that there wasn't one sin in the world that a person couldn't find in Las Vegas, Nevada.

"If we don't have it, then it don't exist," he told her proudly, and then he added. "That's what folks come here for."

She informed him in no uncertain terms that was not her reason for coming to Las Vegas. Then she asked him if he knew Jesus. The smart aleck hack told her that if he hadn't ridden in his cab then he didn't know him. Hattie left him with a Bible verse and a dollar tip. As she exited the cab she heard him utter an unflattering comment about her and her tip. She chalked him up as one more of the city's many hell-bound sinners.

Arriving at her destination, Hattie made the opening session as well as several others before drifting back to the exhibition hall that she had visited the day before. It appeared as though additional booths had been added. She had never seen such an array of religious items and artifacts in her life. As she browsed through the merchandise and service-oriented vendors, Hattie gathered several business cards of merchants whose services she might possibly need for her funeral business. She made a mental note to become more proficient in using the internet on which many of the service vendors seemed to advertise. As for the merchandise for sell, there were so many things to buy that making a decision was difficult. But, she became enthralled by a pair of unique earrings. They were long and dangling and they blinked the name Jesus. She had to have a pair.

Just as she was paying for her purchase she saw Reverend Trees walking toward her. The Lord did answer prayer. He was with an attractive, well dressed older couple and the man looked familiar. As for the reverend he looked great. They hadn't seen each other in more than a week and she was glad to see him. When he flashed an affectionate smile, and gave her a hug in greeting it appeared that he felt the same way.

"Sister Hattie!" He kissed her on the cheek, and then took both of her hands in his. "You could have knocked me over with a feather when I saw you here. Why didn't you let me know that you were coming?"

"I thought that I would surprise you." Hattie's heart was beating like a tom tom. She could hardly believe how happy she felt at seeing him.

"Well you did that all right. Did Miss Fanny come with you?" He looked around the room.

"She's in town." Still smarting from Miss Fanny's rebuffs about coming to the convention, Hattie tried to sound conciliatory. "She's supposed to be coming, but right now she's found something else to occupy her time."

Reverend Trees lifted a questioning brow. "Oh? And what would that be?"

"I'm sorry to say that she's being robbed by what I believe they call a one-armed bandit." She informed him of how she had tried unsuccessfully to save her mother-in-law from the clutches of Vegas.

Reverend Trees shook his head in empathy and then remembering the couple that was with him, he turned to them. "I want you to meet Reverend Carl Journal and his wife Vivian. Carl is the host pastor of this convention."

"This is really an honor." Hattie recognized the evangelist's name as soon as they were introduced. She exchanged vigorous handshakes with the couple. "Reverend Journal I've heard you preach the Word on the radio."

"Well, I'm glad to hear that Sister Collier." Carl Journal had a booming voice. Nature had given him an internal amplifier. At an even six feet, he was about an inch taller than Reverend Trees, but his plump, round body made him appear shorter. His eyes crinkled in the corners as he beamed at Hattie.

"We're just going out to lunch," said Reverend Trees. "I would love for you to join us." He looked at her expectantly.

“Yes, do come.” Vivian Journal was as short and slim as her husband was tall and round. She had a high-pitched, squeaky voice with just the hint of a southern drawl. She was warm and engaging as she hooked her arm through Hattie’s arm. “It would be nice to have another woman along.”

Hattie happily accepted their invitation, excited not only to be with Reverend Trees but in the company of someone of Reverend Journal’s stature as well.

As the two couples steered through the crowd toward the front door, a young man ran up to Reverend Journal. There appeared to be a problem in one of the many committees connected to the convention and the reverend was needed. Reverend Journal turned to Reverend Trees.

“I’m sorry, Samuel, but it looks like you need to come too.”

Visibly disappointed, Reverend Trees turned to Hattie. “I don’t know how long I’ll be. Could you hang around here and wait for me?” His tone was hopeful.

Vivian Journal intervened. “She’ll do no such thing. We could starve to death waiting on you two. You and Carl just run along and I’ll look after Hattie.” The women bid the men farewell and headed out of the building. Still holding on to Hattie’s arm Vivian asked, “If you like chicken salad, I know a place that has the best ever.”

“That sounds good.” Hattie was famished. She hadn’t eaten anything since this morning. “Where are we headed?”

”My house,” she answered.

“You live in Las Vegas?” Hattie couldn’t mask her surprise.

“Sure,” Vivian’s answer was matter-of-fact. “My home is comfortable and quiet, plus the food is delicious. We can talk and get to know one another.”

Two hours later, the women were having a great time. Hattie enjoyed talking to the opinionated minister’s wife. In fact, she and Hattie saw eye-to-eye on a lot of issues. The chatty southern belle was quite impressed with Hattie’s funeral business. She even offered Hattie a few tips on how she could computerize her bookkeeping and make it easier.

When the subject came around to children Vivian revealed that she and her husband had lost their only child when he was struck by a speeding driver who was coming home from an evening of gambling and drinking. Hattie was aghast.

"Tell me, Vivian, how do you stand living in this city with so much sin and corruption on every street corner?"

Vivian chuckled, "Well darlin', sin is not on every corner. We have quite a few God-fearing people who live here. Even though the devil set up shop first, Las Vegas has a thriving Christian community. In fact the convention is all about how the men folk can find ways to evangelize here as well as in their own communities."

"The men folk?" Hattie didn't like the sound of that. "Do you think that saving souls is just for the men?"

"Of course not! I think that we women have our place too."

"I'm glad to hear that." Hattie was hoping that Vivian wasn't one of those shrinking violets. "Because in the short time that I've been here, there is one thing that I'm sure of—this city needs salvation now, and from all of us. On my way flying here I sat next to a Las Vegas atheist and I'm sure that he's not the only one in this town."

"You're right about that," Vivian declared.

"Never mind what's happening on the street," Hattie continued as she worked herself into a mini-sermon. "This place has corrupted my best friends. Both of them have slipped over the line to outright immorality and they don't care who knows it, and Lord help her, since coming here my mother-in-law has completely lost her mind. She's knee deep in the sin of gambling. Before coming here her only vice was playing bingo. Now she's practically a professional gambler and this is only our first full day here. I tell you this is out of control! Something has got to be done about this place."

Vivian was sobered by Hattie's fervor. "What do you propose?"

Hattie had an answer, "We Christians need to shake this town up and show its people the error of their ways."

"Yeah," Vivian agreed. "We need to give them the Word."

Hattie stilled. Vivian could practically see the wheels turning in her head.

"That's it!" Hattie was ecstatic. "We can give them the Word. That's exactly what they need. Lord knows that they don't have it here, even in the hotel room."

Vivian looked puzzled. "What do you mean?"

"When I got to my room yesterday, I looked in the bedside table drawer for a Bible." Hattie paused for dramatic effect. "There was none."

Vivian blinked, apparently searching for the connection.

"So we'll give them the Word," Hattie persisted. "Every man and woman walking into those dens of iniquity needs a Bible."

Vivian digested the idea, and then slowly a smile spread across her face. "Hattie, that's brilliant. Think of all the ladies auxiliary groups at the convention. We can organize them into a small army and give Bibles away."

"I like that!" Hattie's eyes lit up. "We women will be soldiers for the Lord."

"I know a couple of people that could get us media coverage." Vivian's excitement was escalating. "This could be the greatest Bible giveaway in the country."

"That's the truth! Lord knows there's enough work to be done here."

"There's no denying that. I can't wait to tell Carl and Samuel the news." Vivian glanced at her watch. "Maybe we'd better head back to the convention."

Hattie agreed. She was eager to see the look on Reverend Trees' face when she told him what they were thinking about doing. She was also eager to get started. Surely that was her mission from God, the reason that he let her live through that airplane flight and the reason that he sent to Las Vegas. If so, this would be the most significant challenge in her life to date.

"I wish we could start right away, but it just occurred to me that we don't have any Bibles to give way," Hattie lamented.

"No problem. Maybe we can get some donated from the convention. There are usually extra ones at these events."

Later, after returning to the convention Hattie and Vivian found Samuel and Carl and told them about their Bible giveaway idea. Both men greeted it with enthusiasm and offered encouragement. The couples parted company after the convention's last session and Reverend Trees invited Hattie out to dinner. She gladly accepted, excited by the opportunity to be alone with him.

As the shadows of the evening faded into night, Hattie sat in an eloquent dining room across from the man she had admired and respected for so long and thanked the Lord for his blessings. In more ways than one, this trip to Las Vegas had not been in vain. Here she was with Samuel Trees, a handsome, intelligent man of God and she was going to help him fight the battle of good versus evil right here in this den of iniquity. How much better could her life get?

"A penny for your thoughts," Reverend Trees asked as he smiled across the table at her.

Hattie tried not to blush at his intense stare. "I was just thinking what a blessed woman I am," she answered honestly before giving a frustrated sigh. "But I was also wondering where I'm going to get enough Bibles to give away." Reverend Journal had informed her that they had about three hundred extra ones from the convention, but that wasn't enough.

Reverend Trees covered her hand with his. "You know the Lord always provides and this is no exception. He has provided this time too."

"What do you mean?" She quizzed.

"I happen to know where there are 10,000 Bibles which should be more than enough for your give away."

Hattie's eyes widened. "Ten thousand Bibles? That's great! How do we get them?"

He sat back in his chair. "They're in a warehouse that the convention is using for storage, but the reason that they're there is because we're planning on returning them. The convention committee just can't afford that many extra Bibles."

Hattie was disappointed but not disheartened. She was sure that God would provide her with those Bibles somehow.

As though reading her mind, Reverend Trees smiled at her. "Don't worry. The Lord works wonders."

She smiled. "I have no doubt."

With that she settled back to enjoy a wonderful evening. She just knew that a guardian angel would come her way.

CHAPTER 11

If Hattie was going to fight the battle against sin in Las Vegas she would need all of the foot soldiers that she could get, and while the ones at the convention were organizing she needed immediate recruits on the front lines. After praying on it, the Lord answered her entreaty without delay.

She remembered that when she was riding in the cab a few days ago, she had spotted a cross on top of a building that she passed identifying it as a house of the Lord. It seemed to be the only church between her downtown hotel and the unholy Strip. She didn't count all of those so called chapels she had seen as churches. They didn't hold anything inside of them except weddings. Perhaps the parishioners of the church topped with the cross were a bit stronger in their faith. They had to be to exist in the midst of all of this sin. These were the kind of people that she needed.

Having discovered a bus that would take her pass the building on its way to the infamous Strip, Hattie deemed it as more affordable transportation than a cab and boarded the bus. A short while later she stepped off of it right in front of her intended destination. Bible in hand she marched with determination toward the front door of the building, taking a shortcut through a parking lot as she did so. She was surprised to see so many cars parked in the lot on a weekday afternoon. Glancing up at the cross atop the gothic looking structure, she was also surprised to see that the cross that she had noted the other day was revolving and that blazon across it in blinking lights was written the words 'Love God'. She hadn't noticed that before. It was a good sign.

The double doors leading to the building's interior contained beautiful stained glass panels. Hattie was impressed. What she wasn't impressed with was the loud, raucous music that greeted her when she stepped inside of the gaudy red velvet lobby. It was empty except for some slot machines.

"Lord have mercy!" Hattie sputtered taken aback. "What kind of church is this? Is nothing sacred in this town?"

It was evident that the soldiers in this church were serving something other than the Lord. She wanted to meet the pastor who would let something like this be in his church.

As she stepped inside another set of doors it didn't take long for Hattie to realize that The Love God was no church. It was far from it! The light in the interior was muted, but Hattie could clearly see the highly polished bar that dominated the huge room, and the tables covered with velvet table cloths and occupied by men sitting at them guzzling liquor, smoking cigarettes and ogling the nearly nude women swinging from strategically placed poles. There were even scantily clothed women swinging from red velvet ropes suspended in mid air.

Appalled, Hattie clutched her Bible to her chest as if to stave off the devil himself. She could hardly believe that all of this could be happening right beneath the sign of the cross. It was a disgrace! Like an enraged bull with nostril's flaring she charged up to the bar and loudly demanded that the bartender direct her to the owner of the establishment. The round faced man behind the bar was so shocked by the sudden appearance of the wild-eyed woman clutching a Bible that he pointed the way to the back of the club before he could think twice. By the time that he had recovered his senses she had by-passed the bodyguard and disappeared behind the door that separated his boss' office from the rest of the club.

The knock on the locked office door wasn't unexpected as the owner of the establishment went to answer its summons. It was a demanding knock, but he dealt with some demanding people and the person that he was expecting was one of them. Yet in his wildest nightmares he had never expected to come face to face with the person who stood on the other side of his office door. The word shocked wasn't strong enough to describe the simultaneous reaction of both people when they came face to face.

"Larry Smith!" bellowed Hattie.

"Not you!" The beleaguered man from the memorable airplane ride was appalled. He tried to slam the door in her face, but Hattie's adrenaline was pumping and her reflexes proved quicker. Filled with righteous indignation she forced her way past him into his office and then whirled on him in outrage.

"Do you own this place?"

"I sure do, lady, now get out of here!" He rushed to his desk to push the security button.

"You son of Satan!" Hattie's ire could not be contained. "Why in the world would you call this place The Love God and have those precious words written on a cross blazing with lights for all to see?"

"What in the world are you talking about? This is the Love Goddess. There are probably just some bulbs out on our sign. Now leave!"

"You blasphemer!" Hattie raised her Bible and made the sign of the cross just as a burly bodyguard rushed into the room to determine the reason for the commotion. He was stopped momentarily by the sight of a woman who appeared to be trying to assault his boss with a Bible.

"Grab her and get her out of here!" Smith demanded, ready to do the deed himself if needed. "The woman is crazy!"

The body guard grabbed a resistant Hattie who remained undaunted. She was a woman on a mission and she would not be stopped as she waved her Bible in the air with determined purpose.

"I rebuke you in the name of Jesus!"

"Take her out the back way!" A red-faced Larry Smith was so mad he was spewing spittle. What was with this woman? Was she stalking him? "I don't want my customers to see her."

Finding it difficult to handle a wiggling and twisting Bible toting Hattie, the body guard picked her up by the waist. Hattie was not compliant as she held the Word in one hand and the door jamb with the other.

"No weapon formed against me shall prosper!" Hattie declared as her hand was pried from the door jamb and she was unceremoniously dragged out into the hallway. As she was being taken out of the back door a tall, dark haired man with gray steaks in his brown hair was entering it. His startled green eyes met Hattie's as the body guard carried her past him. She raised her Bible to make it clear that her parting words would include him as well as Larry Smith who was in the background directing him to enter and her to get out.

"May the wrath of my Lord and Savior come down on you and this House of Satan! Sweet Jesus! Amen."

Without a word, the body guard set Hattie down firmly on her feet in the alley and slammed the back door in her face. Straightening her dress and adjusting her purse strap on her shoulder, Hattie clutched her Bible and with all of the dignity that she could muster started walking down the alley. It looked as though her job in this city might be more difficult than she thought.

****

"Hattie, I'm not even speaking to you," Bea informed her friend sitting across the table from her. "So if you think that I'm going to help you with anything you're mistaken."

She hadn't seen Hattie since they arrived in Las Vegas three days ago and that was fine with her. If she and Josh hadn't been spotted by her eating lunch in one of the hotel dining rooms it could have been longer. Bea popped a forkful of crab salad in her mouth as a sign that the subject at hand was closed, but Hattie didn't seem to get the message.

"Come on, Bea," Hattie pleaded. "You know that you can't stay mad with me long. "I need soldiers in this fight against the infidels in this city. Time cannot be wasted. The fires of hell are ready to ravage this city soon."

Bea rolled her eyes at her, "I don't care." She popped another spoonful of salad into her mouth.

"Well I do." Josh transferred his full attention to Hattie. "I've lived in this town for twenty-five years and I can't disagree with you that it's going to hell in a hand basket, but what would you suggest be done to turn the tide?"

"I don't believe that you're encouraging this lunacy!" The last thing Bea wanted was for her new man to get caught up in one of Hattie's crazy schemes.

The smile that Josh flashed at her was patient. "If there's a way that I can help the town that took such good care of me I'd like to do it." He turned back to Hattie. "What do you have in mind?"

"Oh, God," Bea groaned. She couldn't wait to hear this one.

Hattie ignored her and concentrated on Josh. "I say that the people in this town need the word of the Lord. They need the Bible to guide them to the path of righteousness."

"And where do you plan on getting these Bibles?"

Josh's question appeared to take Hattie by surprise as she looked at him blankly. "What do you mean?"

"These Bibles that you're talking about, where are they?

Bea looked at Hattie with amusement. "Yes, where are they?"

"Uh, do you mean actual Bibles?" Hattie hadn't been prepared for that question.

"What other kind of Bibles are there?" Bea chided. It was about time that someone challenged Hattie. She glanced at Josh who seemed sincere about helping Hattie. The man was totally clueless about what he might be getting into. Okay, then let him learn the hard way. She finished her salad.

Hattie didn't appreciate Bea's sarcasm. She would show her. She searched her mind for an answer to Josh's question and then the answer came to her.

"They have Bibles that they're giving away at the convention. Reverend Trees said that they had ordered too many. He said that they have 10,000 of them that they'll have to return."

"Are they the big ones or the pocket sized?" Josh was obviously interested.

Hattie perked up, giving Bea a triumphant glance before answering. "They're the pocket sized. They'll fit in the purse or the pocket."

"Then I'll buy all 10,000 and donate them to you to give away. You think that Las Vegas needs the Word, then give it to them." Josh sat back to enjoy the look of joy that appeared on Hattie's face. Out of the corner of his eye he could see Bea shake her head in disagreement.

"Oh Josh, thank you!" Hattie squealed. Maybe Bea didn't appreciate this man's generosity, but she did. "And I bet that you can buy them from the convention wholesale. The reverend will see to that." Hattie rose, excited and scared that Josh might change his mind if she didn't make a quick exit. "I'm going to talk to him and see if he'll do that." She backed away from the table. "I'm sorry that I interrupted you two. I was just down because of what happened at that Love Goddess place that I told you about." Her eyes lit up with a thought. "As a matter of fact that would be the perfect place to start giving them away."

"Maybe you can notify the press that you're going to give a press conference out in front of the place and let the world know what you're doing." Bea regretted the words as soon as they came out of her mouth, especially when she saw that Hattie had taken her seriously.

"That's a great idea, Bea!" Hattie could hardly contain herself. "Vivian Journal said she knew a couple of media people. After I call the reverend we'll contact the newspaper and the TV and radio stations." She turned to leave and was nearly knocked off her feet as she bumped into Miss Fanny. "Miss Fanny! I've been looking for you. Why haven't you been answering my phone calls?"

"I didn't want to hear your fussing," Miss Fanny responded. She turned to smile at Bea and Josh. "So you two came up for air, huh? How are you doing?"

"Fine, Miss Fanny," Bea was glad to see her. She had actually missed her wise cracks over these past few days.

"Hello." Josh gave her a sparkling smile. He liked her a lot. She reminded him of his late mother. "Have you been enjoying yourself?"

"I'm having a ball!" Miss Fanny couldn't begin to explain how much fun she was having. "I've hit every hotel around here and I'm headed toward the Strip now. Did ya'll know that some of these hotels give away free money to start you out gambling? Of course, some of them don't. The misers!"

"You need to be worrying about getting straight with the Lord, not about getting free money at some hotel!" Hattie warned. "You said that you would be going to the convention and I haven't seen hide nor hair of you there. As a matter of fact, I hardly see you at all. You come in and out of our hotel room like a tornado."

"I've got things to do," sniffed Miss Fanny. She had tried to avoid Hattie as much as possible, going to their hotel room when she thought she wouldn't be there or when she thought that she might be asleep. What dumb luck that she would bump into her down here.

"Obviously praying is not one of them," Hattie retorted.

"That's not true. I say 'Thank you Lord' every time I win some money." Miss Fanny started pass her.

"You're being corrupted like the rest of these sinners in this town," Hattie called after her.

"See you Bea and Josh." Miss Fanny disappeared into the crowd leaving a steaming Hattie staring after her.

"That woman is too close to the Pearly Gates to be knocking on Satan's door now," she muttered loudly. "I can't let her go down now."

The situation was urgent. There wasn't a second to lose. Sin City had to be saved.

****

Connie couldn't believe what she was seeing. David and she had been relaxing in the limo headed back to their hotel from the Strip when she looked out of the window and saw Hattie. She was standing on the sidewalk talking into a microphone held by a local television reporter. What in the world was happening?

Ordering the limo driver to stop, David and she had jumped out and headed toward the small cluster of people observing the spectacle. It was being held in front of a building topped by a revolving cross. When they reached the sidewalk to Connie's surprise Bea and Josh were among the spectators. She tugged at Bea's sleeve.

"What's going on? Is Hattie doing publicity for the convention?"

Bea shook her head no and proceeded to recount for Connie her encounter with Hattie the day before and Josh's offer to buy the Bibles for distribution.

I had no idea that she could get all of this together so quickly." There was disbelief in her voice. She and Josh had gone out on the town alone yesterday evening and she hadn't spoken to Connie until now. "Last night before Josh and I went out Hattie brought Reverend Trees over to pick up the check to pay for the Bibles. An hour ago she called and asked me and Josh to meet her here in front of this place. We came here and found all of this." Bea spread her hands to indicate her surroundings.

Connie's eyes widened. "You mean she did this in one day?" She couldn't help but be impressed.

"It looks like there's a fire burning in your friend about those Bibles," Josh noted.

"She's really going off the deep end this time." Bea was used to Hattie's extremes, but on home turf, not on vacation.

"She's taking her insanity to a new level, that's for sure," Connie agreed.

"Who's the dude over there talking to the police?" David gestured to a man standing in the background near the entrance of the building in front of which the interview was taking place. He was waving his arms wildly, pointing to the commotion on the sidewalk, visibly upset about what was happening.

“That looks like the guy on the airplane!” Connie squinted to scrutinize the irate man. Bea confirmed her observation.

“It’s him. That’s his place over there. He and Hattie had a confrontation yesterday. From what she told us she stormed into this club, found out that he owned it and got up in his face. He threw her out.”

“Sshh, let’s listen,” Josh urged. “She’s talking about the Bible give away.”

All attention turned toward Hattie, who was dressed in her Sunday best, clutching her Bible and was handling herself before the cameras like a pro. She had started calling the media late last night and early this morning. She hadn’t known what to expect until she got here. Only one television station had showed up, but she was pleased. It showed what could be done with God on your side. One was all that she needed to get the word out and that was exactly what she was doing.

After explaining who she was and why she was in Las Vegas and how she as a Christian felt about the vice around her, it was time for the big announcement.

“I want to tell all of the good people of Las Vegas that help is on the way in overcoming this sin and corruption. Tomorrow at high noon, right under this cross that should represent the good Lord, we will be giving away 10,000…”

The piercing sound of a horn from a passing big rig truck drowned out Hattie’s words for a second. The crowd that had gathered who hadn’t heard the announcement’s conclusion looked at each other in confusion. The reporter thanked Hattie and she and the cameraman packed up their equipment and left. The onlookers dispersed, a ripple of excitement following them as they went to spread the word about what they thought that they had heard Hattie announce.

Bea and Connie chided Hattie for her foolishness. Larry Smith rushed up to her and threatened to have her arrested if she came within ten feet of his establishment again. However, confident in her mission and armed with the knowledge that she wasn’t trespassing by standing on the public sidewalk, Hattie blessed him again with her Bible and told him that she would pray for his soul. Amid a string of profanity from the ungrateful man, her friends quickly whisked her away in the limo and took her back with them to their hotel.

That evening while Bea, Connie and their dates were enjoying another night out, and Miss Fanny was heaven knows where, Hattie tried hard to stay awake to see the interview she'd given today on the news. She had alerted Reverend Trees who had said that he would watch it too. He also promised that he would see that volunteers delivered the Bibles the next day and that they would help give them away.

Unfortunately, the reverend and Hattie were both asleep when the interview was broadcast. If they had been awake they would have heard the newscaster misspeak when he invited the people of Las Vegas to the $10,000 give away at noon the next day. It was to be held in the parking lot next to The Love Goddess Club, and there were no strings attached.

CHAPTER 12

Hattie woke up the morning of the Bible giveaway with a feeling of nervous anticipation. Today was the day that she would take a bite out of Satan's evil plan for this city by arming 10,000 sinners with the Word of God. Las Vegas was a microcosm of the world and while she couldn't save everybody in it, she was definitely going to try to save some of the souls in this place. The determined crusader practically leaped out of bed, partly out of enthusiasm and partly to beat her mother-in-law to the bathroom before the older woman began her forage into the gamblers' dens.

Miss Fanny was lying in bed flipping through the television channels when Hattie hustled past her bedroom.

"Why are you hopping around like a chicken with its head cut off?" Her mother-in-law inquired.

"And why are you still here in the hotel room?" Hattie retorted. Shutting the bathroom door behind her, a second later she threw it open again and hollered out. "Don't tell me that you lost all of your money?"

"I certainly did not. I'm just starting out late today, that's all. That hot sun can take its toll."

Shrugging her agreement, Hattie closed the door again. Thirty minutes later she was dressed and collecting her purse. She was ready to meet some of the volunteers from the convention who would help her battle sin. They would convene at a parking lot close to The Love Goddess. What better place to give away 10,000 copies of God's word than near the business of an admitted atheist?

As she was leaving, she issued her mother-in-law a challenge. "Miss Fanny, you haven't spent one single minute at the convention. The least you could do is come with me to help with the Bible giveaway."

The older woman made no response. Her eyes stayed glued on the television screen as she turned up the volume

"I can take a hint," Hattie snapped. With that she stormed from the room, slamming the door behind her. Miss Fanny didn't notice her leaving the suite as she listened intently to the two talking heads on the morning news.

"Well the city is in for a pleasant surprise," one of the anchors chatted happily. "As news reporter, Rita Jameson reported yesterday, the whole town is buzzing with the news that The Love Goddess Club is sponsoring a $10,000 give away. Some of you, who may remember the club from several violent incidents that have occurred there in the past year, might be surprised at the spokesperson for the giveaway."

Miss Fanny let out a yelp of recognition when Hattie's face popped up on the screen. There she was hanging on to a microphone making some kind of announcement. What was her daughter-in-law doing on television talking about giving away money? Whose money was it and where did she get it? More importantly, if she had it why would she give it away?

"Has that woman lost what little sense that she's got?" Miss Fanny grumbled before shouting out, "Hattie!"

Getting no answer she got up from the bed and checked the suite. Hattie was gone. Miss Fannie settled back in front of the television where the anchor continued.

"So far we have no details on the rules of the giveaway, but news of such an unusual promotion has prompted the interest of at least one national media source."

Miss Fanny frowned. Something wasn't right. Hattie had done some strange things in her life, but giving away her money had never been one of them. She called Bea.

After several rings, her call was answered. Miss Fanny dispensed with the greeting and came straight to the point.

"Bea , are you aware of what your crazy friend is up to?"

Bea chuckled. "You must be talking about the giveaway."

Fanny couldn't believe her ears. "Lord have mercy! Is everyone around here crazy? You mean you know about this and didn't try to stop her?"

"It's okay, Miss Fanny. She's determined to do something to save the souls in this city. At least it will keep her occupied."

Fanny was astonished. "Are you kidding? Hattie is not a rich woman. She can't afford to be passing out 10,000 anything!"

Bea laughed. "Miss Fanny, you live with Hattie so you understand her religious zeal. She believes in what she's doing."

Miss Fanny wasn't convinced. "I've got zeal too, but I'm not going around giving away my money."

Bea replied, "She's not spending a thing. Josh donated the money for her to buy the books."

"What books?" Miss Fannie replied. "Who's talking about books? This fool is giving away $10,000."

Correcting her, Bea recounted the conversation that she and Josh had had with Hattie. "And that's when Josh gave her a check to purchase the Bibles," she concluded.

Miss Fanny gave a frustrated groan. "Perhaps you two love birds should come up for air. I was watching the news a few minutes ago and they announced that Hattie was giving away money. They had her on TV, just as big as day talking about how she was giving away $10,000 today. It came out of her own mouth!"

"That can't be," Bea sputtered. "I know. I was there. We were there."

The telephone call was interrupted by a knock on the bathroom door where Bea had been applying her makeup. "Come in, Josh," she called out.

The door opened and Josh stood in the doorway. One look at his face confirmed for Bea what Miss Fanny had been telling her.

He sighed. "We've got a problem."

Less than an hour later, Bea, Josh, Connie and David were in a taxi on their way to find Hattie. Josh had verified not only Miss Fanny's story, but he stated that the mistake about the giveaway had escalated to Hattie having become the spokesperson for club owner, Larry Smith. It was he who was being given credit for giving the money away. Both Bea and Connie had tried to call Hattie and warn her of the error, but she hadn't answered her cell phone.

When they arrived at the site near the Love Goddess Club where the event was scheduled to take place, there was a throng of people. Hattie was nowhere in sight. The group decided to split up. Bea and Josh worked their way through one end of the crowd. David and Connie worked the other end. As they pressed through the crowd, people were buzzing about the possibility of someone winning the money.

Connie's cell phone rang. She answered anxiously. It was Bea.

"Make your way to the east side of the building as quick as you can."

David and Connie elbowed their way to Bea's location where Josh was already stationed. It was there that they saw Hattie. Members of the media had encircled her. One reporter had a microphone shoved in her face.

"It's the reporter from Info Hollywood!" Bea explained. "He's interviewing Hattie." She wasn't quite sure if that was good or bad.

The group pushed its way close enough to hear Hattie's protest. "I don't know nothing about giving away any $10,000. I'm doing the Lord's work. Anybody who wants a word from Him can get that free." She held up a small white Bible with raised gold lettering.

The aggressive reporter thrust the microphone closer. "Mrs. Collier, I'm looking at an estimated crowd of at least a thousand and it's growing by the second. Are you saying that you got these people here under false pretenses?"

"No, I didn't say that," she protested.

He wouldn't be deterred. "How long have you and Larry Smith been planning this publicity stunt? What's your acquaintance with Smith and how did he pick you for his front woman?"

"Front woman?" Hattie was incensed. "I don't know what you're talking about. I'm a decent, Christian woman. I don't have a thing to do with Larry Smith!" She jabbed the reporter in the chest with a finger. "You'd better stop that lie about me and that godless heathen doing anything together! I work for one person and his name is…"

She pointed to the dangling earrings that she wore and they started blinking Jesus. The reporter took a step back, surprised by the unique jewelry.

Turning to the camera he went from his exclusive breaking news story voice to his serious world shaking issue voice.

"And there you have it, folks, Hattie Collier is denying that she announced a $10,000 give away at this very spot just 24 hours ago. Later in the show we'll try to get an interview with Larry Smith, the owner of the Love Goddess Club and the reported brains behind this supposed giveaway. This is Harper Ferry reporting for Info Hollywood, live in Las Vegas."

As soon as the cameras were turned off, Bea, Connie and Miss Fanny tried to reach Hattie, but Vivian Journal appeared out of nowhere and pulled her away from them.

"It's time for the giveaway," she hollered above the din.

"Hattie!" Bea called out to her. "I need to talk to you."

"After the giveaway," Hattie tossed over her shoulder.

She followed Vivian to a small podium that had been set up in a vacant lot beside the Love Goddess Club. Vivian handed Hattie a bull horn. After taking a moment to collect herself, she raised it to her lips.

"Ladies and gentlemen, my name is Mrs. Hattie Collier and my fellow Christians and I are here from our annual church convention with something that will help each and every one of you."

A loud roar of approval rose from the crowd. Buoyed by the enthusiasm, Hattie smiled at Vivian and the Sisters of Mercy Women's Auxiliary standing nearby. She pushed on.

"Now that's the kind of excitement for the Lord's Word that he likes. It shows that you know that what we're giving away is better than any money, and I believe we'll be able to accommodate everyone here today."

Hattie flashed another smile, but she noticed that the mood of the people had shifted. They seemed confused as they whispered to one another. Hattie wasn't quite sure what had caused the change, but she continued. She pointed to the group of women dressed in white. The Sisters of Mercy were standing in back of dozens of large cardboard boxes.

"I know each of you will be pleased as the ladies from our convention pass out our love offering." With that the ladies dipped into the boxes, bringing up armloads of Bibles. They began handing them out to the nearest bystanders. People surged forward.

"Be patient," she told them brightly. "There are enough for everyone."

A few moments later someone from the crowd shouted, "What the hell is this?"

Someone else called out, "Are they're using Bibles for lottery tickets?"

"Maybe the money is between the pages of the Bible," another person suggested,

The protest grew as people took Bibles and passed them back to others in the crowd who rifled through the pages and found nothing. Hattie and Vivian looked at each other uneasily as the crowd began to grow hostile.

One man held a Bible up in the air and yelled, "Where's the $10,000?"

"What are they talking about?" Vivian was frantic. "What $10,000?"

Hattie briefly recounted to her what the reporter had said. "But I didn't take it seriously."

A wide-eyed Vivian glanced at the angry crowd. "Obviously they did."

By now there was mass confusion. People were talking excitedly, others were laughing at the absurdity of it all and still others were cursing out loud. Hattie tried to calm the storm.

"You might have heard something about some money…"

"Yeah, $10,000!" Someone hollered.

"Where is it you fraud?"

"Cheat!"

"Crook!"

As if summoned by the descriptions, Larry Smith appeared. He fought his way through the angry crowd, which by now was tossing Bibles to the ground as well as at the ladies who were dodging them like bullets. He was trembling with rage as he got in Hattie's face.

"I've called the cops," He growled at her. "I told you yesterday that you had better not come on my property, but you didn't listen. Let's see how you feel when you go to jail for trespassing."

More fearful of the unfriendly crowd than of him, Hattie glared at the red-faced man. "For your information this is public property, Mr. Smith."

Larry sneered. "Oh yeah, we'll see about that! I'm going to throw you and your little elves in jail."

No sooner had the pronouncement been made then the police sirens could be heard blaring as police cars came to a halt at the giveaway site. Where there had been only two policemen on hand previously to contain the crowd, half dozen officers now spilled out of their cars to join them. The majority of the spectators started walking away in disgust, with and without Bibles.

While Hattie and Larry Smith continued to argue, her friends tried to work their way over to where they stood, but Harper Ferry and his cameraman beat them to the feuding duo. They watched as the annoying reporter thrust the microphone into Larry's Smith face.

"Mr. Smith, just what was your part in today's event? Are you involved in this so-called Bible giveaway?"

Smith whirled on the reporter. His face was a mask of rage. He spewed fire. Tiny flecks of spittle settled onto Ferry's nose. "I don't give a damn about this Bible crap or this loony woman. And if you say different I'll sue the shit out of you! Now get that thing out of my face before I wrap it around your neck!" He pushed the mike away.

Trying not to look intimidated, Ferry backed away from the menacing figure and faced the camera. "And that's the official word from Las Vegas club owner, Larry Smith. This is Harper Ferry, for Info Hollywood."

Wrapping up quickly, Ferry and his cameraman made a hasty retreat just as a policeman walked up to the club owner.

"Hey, Larry," he greeted the man with familiarity.

"Larry?" Bea echoed. "Do you two know each other?"

"What is this some sort of police conspiracy?" Connie wanted to know.

"Oh great!" Larry threw his hands in the air. "She's got her fellow loonies here."

Hattie addressed the officer. "Are you in cahoots with him? Do you know each other on a personal basis?"

The officer gave Hattie a quizzical look before turning back to the club owner. "What seems to be the problem here?"

"This is the problem." Smith flung his arms out wide indicating everything around him. "This woman is trespassing after I warned her just yesterday not to do it."

Hattie protested. "Officer, I am Mrs. Hattie Collier, and if I was standing on his property, I would be trespassing, but I am not. This empty lot is next door to his club's parking lot and I think that it is owned by the city."

The officer took out a writing pad and listened patiently as everyone around him began speaking at once, trying to explain about the Bibles, the money giveaway and their right to be on public property. Finally the officer had had enough.

"Everybody shut up!"

When order resumed, Larry Smith reached into his pocket and pulled out a folded sheet of paper. He handed it to the policeman who scanned it.

"Sorry, ma'am," the officer addressed Hattie. "This is his property. It says here that he bought it a few weeks ago. If he wants to press charges, I'll have to take you in for trespassing."

"You've got to be kidding!" cried Hattie. "You're going to arrest me?"

"In a heartbeat," Smith scoffed. He jabbed a thumb toward the squad car. "Take her ass to jail."

Josh stepped forward and addressed the policeman. "I'm sure that a mistake has been made here, officer."

He handed his driver's license to the man. The officer read his name and his entire demeanor changed. He smiled and began to pump Josh's hand.

"Mr. Pierce, It's a pleasure to meet you in person. I've always wanted to meet the man who has done so much for the Police Athletic League in this city."

Larry groaned in frustration, "What is this? Did the woman bring her own cheerleading squad? "

Ignoring him the officer continued to address Josh. "I wish we'd met under different circumstances."

"I wish we had too," Josh agreed, "but right now I'd like to intercede for Mrs. Collier and let you know that if there has been any violation of the law on her part I'm sure that it was a mistake. I can vouch for her credibility and integrity. Surely this can be worked out."

Nodding, the officer handed the license back to Josh and then turned back to Hattie. "Well, Mrs. Collier, I'll tell you what. I still need to take you to the station so that we can sort this thing out. Do you have a permit to hold this gathering?"

"I bet that she doesn't," Larry sounded confident. "That's another charge against her. Now would you remove her from my property? She's a thorn in my side."

"And you're still going to hell," Hattie assured him. She was ready to take this godless demon on.

"Same to you," Larry snapped before turning to the officer. "And I'll be down to press those charges." He stormed back across the nearly empty lot toward his club.

The officer assisted an unhappy Hattie into the squad car ignoring the loud protest of her friends and supporters. The Sisters of Mercy began a spontaneous rendition of "Ain't Gonna Let Nobody Turn Me Around" led by Vivian. The policeman advised her friends where she would be taken.

Josh and David escorted the ladies back to the limo, ready to follow Hattie to the station. Sitting in the backseat of the squad car, Hattie peered out of the window at Vivian Journal and the Sisters of Mercy. Vivian's face was grim, but as her eyes met Hattie's eyes Vivian gave her two thumbs up. Hattie returned the gesture. They both knew that the Bible giveaway had been a wonderful idea that was meant to bless the city of Las Vegas.

"We may have lost this battle, Satan," Hattie whispered to her nemesis as the car rolled away, "but before it's over we will win this war."

CHAPTER 13

Sitting in a small cluttered office in the Las Vegas police station, Hattie appeared to be calm as she rang off her cell phone after calling Bea and Connie. She wanted to let them know that she was still in the detective's office being questioned. They had followed her to the station and were downstairs waiting for her. She glanced at the burley police detective who waited patiently for her to finish her call. Sitting behind an ugly, metal desk was Detective James Norwalsky. She had been in his office for nearly an hour. When she disconnected he looked at her suspiciously.

"Okay, Mrs. Collier, you've had your one telephone call. Your constitutional rights have been protected. Believe me I would be the last person to take them away from you."

"That's good to hear, Detective. As I told you before, I am a servant of the Lord and a citizen of the United States of America and I know my rights. I don't appreciate being interrogated like some criminal." Hattie was indignant and she didn't like the man's sarcastic attitude.

"Sorry that you feel that way, but a complaint has been lodged against you. Mr. Smith said that you were trespassing on his property, plus you can't produce a permit for that gathering."

"The only thing I am guilty of is being a soldier in the army of my Lord and Savior and an enemy of the devil. If that's a crime then so be it."

Norwalsky studied her tight expression. "Well, like I've told you before, Smith said that he's going to press charges because you and your little helpers..."

"The Sisters of Mercy."

"Whatever," Norwalsky retorted. "But the fact is that you didn't stay off of his property like he told you to do and you need a permit for gatherings."

Hattie gave a frustrated sigh. "Detective Norcocky..."

"It's Norwalsky..."

"I've been in here with you for much too long. So fine me for not having a permit and if Mr. Smith is going to press charges then let him do it. Is he here?"

"I assume that he's on his way. Right now I'm just trying to understand why you and those women were out there without a permit and what did you hope to prove?"

Hattie rolled her eyes skyward. "For the umpteenth time, I was trying to give away Bibles to the sinners in this town, and I can assure you that's a mighty big order."

"Then where did this $10,000 come in that people expected to get?" Norwalsky demanded.

Hattie shrugged. "I don't know! The Sisters and I are giving away 10,000 Bibles, not 10,000 dollars. This is ridiculous! Why do you keep asking me stuff that I don't know anything about? My answer is not going to change."

The detective looked skeptical as he stood and walked to the front of the desk. He settled his large frame on the edge. His blue eyes traveled over Hattie slowly, noting her conservative dress and the Jesus jewelry that she was wearing. He leaned toward her menacingly.

"What's the scam, lady? What are you really up to?"

Hattie leaned into him and met his eyes without blinking. "I'm up to serving my Lord and Master. And it's a job that I do quite well."

She was disappointed in Detective Norwalsky. He had seemed so nice at first when he seated her at his desk. That impression had proved to be false. As the questioning progressed he had turned from Dr. Jekyll into Mr. Hyde, leaving her to wonder if she needed a lawyer. She didn't know where this was headed and it was with that thought in mind that she had called her friends. She wanted to let them know what was happening, hoping that they could help her before she got thrown into the slammer.

Norwalsky started to respond to Hattie's declaration, but a commotion coming from the other side of the door halted his words. Curious, he went to check on its source. Opening the door, he looked into the hallway. Coming toward him was the duty officer with two older women in tow. They didn't look happy and neither did the officer.

"Detective Norwalsky…" the officer started to address him.

Holding up his hand, Norwalsky stopped the procession several feet from where he stood. "I don't know what the problem is," he said to the officer, "but handle it. I'm with somebody."

The young policeman stepped closer to him and whispered into Norwalsky's ear as he gestured toward the two women. "They say they're here to represent Hattie Collier, the woman that you're questioning. They were raising all kind of hell at my desk, so I figured since she's not been formally arrested…"

"Oh Lord!" Bea shrieked. "Did I hear you say that Hattie's been arrested?"

Norwalsky glanced at the woman and then returned his attention to the officer. He whispered, "What do you mean they represent her? Who are they?"

"I would bet my life that they're no lawyers" the officer grunted.

"Did I hear you say no lawyers? What do you mean no lawyers?" Connie demanded. "Let's get this straight. If Hattie wants legal representation, you'd better make sure that she gets it."

Bea and Connie looked at the two officers defiantly.

"He didn't say that she doesn't get a lawyer," Norwalsky tried to explain. "He said that you aren't lawyers." These ladies needed to improve their eavesdropping skills. "By the way, who are you people?"

"I'm Mrs. Bea Bell and this is Mrs. Connie Palmer. Our friend, Hattie Collier, called us a few minutes ago and said that she's being railroaded into prison. We demand to see her right now!"

The words had hardly left Bea's mouth when Hattie, alerted by her friends' voices, peered into the hall. The three women reunited as though Hattie had been sentenced to life imprisonment. Then, before Norwalsky could stop her, Hattie snatched Bea and Connie into the room with her and slammed the door, leaving the two policemen standing outside.

With a heavy sigh, the beleaguered detective instructed the officer to go back to his duties. Inside the room, Bea was indignant.

"Are you under arrest or not?" She wrapped a protective arm around Hattie.

"Who is this fool who's questioning you?"

"I'm that fool," Norwalsky answered coolly as he entered the room "Detective James Norwalsky. Mrs. Collier is being detained. No one is under arrest—yet." He looked pointedly at all three women.

"What do you mean by that?" It was Connie's turn to get indignant.

"You did say that Larry Smith wanted to press charges," Hattie reminded him.

Crossing her arms tightly, Bea glared at him. "I'll have you know that the three of us are professionals in the field of investigation."

"Oh yeah?" Norwalsky gave a sarcastic grunt, but Bea wasn't finished.

"Now, I demand to know who Larry Smith thinks he is and what Hattie Collier is doing at this police station?"

"And I insist that my friends stay in here with me while you grill me or I'm not saying another word," Hattie threatened.

"He's been grilling you?" Connie gave a disapproving frown.

"He sure has, and with no lawyer present."

"Nazi," Bea hissed at the detective.

Norwalsky rubbed his eyes wearily. It was late and he was too tired to battle with these women. "All right, ladies, you can stay, but no talking."

Satisfied, Bea and Connie settled into two metal chairs placed against the wall. Norwalsky returned his attention to Hattie.

"Let's get on with it shall we? As I said before, Mr. Smith made the request that you move from in front of his property…"

"Did he? I don't remember."

"Well according to him he did."

"I was on the public street," Hattie insisted, "and I don't see how he had a thing to do with what I do on the public street."

"Now just who is Mr. Smith to the police that they seem to know him so intimately?" Connie wanted to know.

Norwalsky ignored her as he concentrated on Hattie. "You were on his property when you were giving away Bibles."

Hattie shifted in her seat. "I didn't know that he owned that vacant lot..."

"Now you do." The detective looked smug.

Hattie's eyes narrowed. She didn't like Norwalsky one bit. She was trying to help this city solve its vice and corruption problem and he wasn't being appreciative at all.

"I am trying to help you people," she snapped.

"Oh? And who are you to decide what the people in this city need?"

"I am a foot soldier for my Lord and that's who helps me make my decisions."

"You tell him, Hattie!" Bea hadn't been on board with what her friend had been planning, but this detective was rubbing her the wrong way.

Norwalsky's bushy eyebrows shot up. "So God recruited you personally, huh?"

"Yes, he did when I was five years old and dipped in the baptismal pool by my father."

"Amen!" Bea concurred.

"Now Larry Smith he's the owner of that club, right?" Connie asked again. This time she wasn't going to be ignored. It was Hattie who answered.

"Yes. He's the same guy that was sitting next to Miss Fanny and me on the airplane, remember?"

Connie nodded. "Yes, I do."

Bea grunted. "He obviously has some clout around here with the police since the cops know him on a first-name basis."

"You've got that right," Connie agreed.

"Ladies…" Norwalsky tried unsuccessfully to interrupt.

"So he claims to own both properties, huh?" Connie started putting the puzzle pieces together.

"That's what he says," Hattie was still skeptical.

"And that's all that he needed to have the police nab you," Bea mumbled thoughtfully.

"Sounds like a setup to me," Connie concluded.

"It's the work of the devil," Hattie declared, "and I fell right into the trap like a…"

"Hot damn, ladies!" The detective exploded. "Would you please be quiet? If you don't stop yapping and let me do my job, I'll throw you two out of here." He pointed to Connie and Bea. "This little hen party is over!"

The three women looked stunned. Without a word, Bea stood and stepped out of the office, slamming the door so hard behind her that the pictures on the walls shifted.

"I know you weren't talking to us like that!" Hattie's eyes were slits.

Connie turned on the detective. "Tell me you didn't just call us hens? Because if you did, we're going to report your sexist behind this instant."

Hattie was fuming. "Each one of us is old enough to be your mother. You best show some respect"

"Norwalsky looked unapologetic, but he complied. "Okay, I apologize. Can we get on with this? " He turned to Connie, "And Mrs. Perkins…"

"Mrs. Palmer." Connie was doubly insulted that the man didn't remember her name.

"Palmer, Pattycake, whatever, maybe you should step outside with your friend."

Sputtering, Connie was about to give him a piece of her mind when Bea re-entered the room. She held her cell phone out to Norwalsky. Her voice was granite.

"My son, Detective Bryant Bell of the Indianapolis Police Department would like to speak to you."

Looking surprised, Norwalsky hesitated for a moment and then he took the phone from Bea. "Detective Norwalsky"

The three women watched him haughtily as they listened to the conversation on their end. Bryant must have asked him what was happening as the officer recounted the Bible fiasco and the reason for Hattie's presence at the police station. Bryant said something to him again and the detective answered in the affirmative. There was a little more small talk, and then he returned the telephone to Bea who bid her son a thank you and a goodbye while the fuming detective retreated to the other side of his desk. He dropped down into a well worn swivel chair.

"I don't need this," Norwalsky mumbled to himself. His words started another torrent of comments as the three women all spoke at once.

"You called us hens."

"I've been down here for over an hour!"

"I refuse to be insulted by you…"

While pandemonium reined, the office door flew open and the young officer who had escorted Bea and Connie to Norwalsky reappeared.

"Sir! We've got a big problem."

"Tell me something that I don't know!" Norwalsky grumbled. Exasperated, he swiped his hand down his face.

The officer stepped inside and said in a loud whisper, "Lieutenant Scott told me to come and get you. There's something going on outside and he says it's about her." His eyes darted to Hattie.

"I can hear you." Hattie informed them both. She was tired of being pushed around.

Giving an exasperated sigh, Norwalsky had gotten up from his desk to follow the officer when Lieutenant Scott burst into the already cramped office.

"Detective Norwalsky, what the hell is going on?" The room nearly quaked with the force of his anger. It was obvious to the three women that this man's bite might be as bad as his bark.

Lieutenant Scott was six foot six and had to weigh at least 300 pounds. His presence seemed to suck the air right out of the room as he boomed.

"I've been on the force for nearly thirty years. I've seen a lot in my time, but never have I've seen anything like I am witnessing today."

Norwalsky snapped to attention at his lieutenant's entrance. He started to explain the presence of Hattie Collier and her friends. "Uh, it seems that…"

His mouth snapped closed as the angry officer brushed past him, grabbed the cord to the blinds at the window and quickly raised them. Sunlight streamed into the stuffy room that overlooked the front of the building. He turned to Norwalsky.

"Would you like to explain this?" He pointed out of the window.

Confused, Norwalsky looked at the lieutenant then looked down onto the street. Not intimidated by either man, Hattie, Bea and Connie crowded both of them at the window.

On the street below, in front of the police station was a single line of women standing side by side, shoulder to shoulder. They were dressed in white and wore white lace handkerchiefs on their heads.

"The Sisters of Mercy," Hattie noted in awe. Tears welled in her eyes at the sight of them standing in solidarity in support of her cause.

There were at least a hundred of them. The line stretched for a city block. They were silent in their commanding presence as they stood pointing to their dangling earrings that blinked the word Jesus. In the middle of the cluster of women one stood carrying a sign that read: FREE HATTIE COLLIER.

Norwalsky was stunned. "What the hell?"

"It's not about that, detective," explained Hattie. "It's about the other direction." She hollered down to the sign holder through the sealed window. "Bless you, Vivian!"

Lieutenant Scott was not amused. He whirled on Hattie, pointing a finger in her face.

"Listen lady, you'd better go down there and tell those Mercy Angels or whatever you call them to move on or else all of you troublemakers are going to jail."

"Oh no he didn't put his finger in your face!" Bea hit speed dial to reconnect with her son.

"I'm calling my attorney," Connie warned as she whipped out her cell phone. "We'll see about this."

Hattie had only one question as she looked up into the veteran police officer's face. "Are you going to throw me in jail or not? If you are, I'm not afraid. Not only do I have those women down there on my side, but I've got somebody more powerful than you standing by me. I've got—." Dramatically, she pointed to the dangling earrings that were like those worn by the women in the street below. They started blinking, Jesus.

Stunned, the lieutenant looked at the earrings in astonished awe. He turned to Norwalsky who looked just as amazed. "Do something about this."

As if in a trance Lieutenant Scott turned to leave, shouting at the duty officer who stood transfixed by the earrings. "Don't you have something to do, Cornwall?"

The officer scrambled out of the door ahead of him. The lieutenant slammed the door behind them. Once again the pictures on the walls swayed.

While Bea updated her son on the latest insult and Connie consulted her attorney to see if a lawsuit could be levied against the

Las Vegas police department, Hattie stood at the window waving her arms to her supporters below. Unfortunately, they couldn't see or hear her. Wearily, Norwalsky dropped down in his chair in surrender.

"Okay ladies, you win."

All three women halted their actions as they turned their attention to the over stressed policeman.

"Mr. Smith hasn't come to press charges. Mrs. Collier, you can pay your fine for the permit and then go back to your hotel."

"I'll call you back, Bryant," Bea whispered hurriedly into her phone and then hung up.

"He's letting us out of here," Connie told her lawyer. She hung up too.

Hattie turned from the window and gave him a strained smile. "Thank you, Detective Norcocky."

Norwalky groaned. "Just leave!"

Hurriedly, all three women headed for the door. Norwalsky called after Hattie.

"I've got your contact information, Mrs. Collier. If he does press charges, I'm coming after you."

The door slammed for the last time that day as Norwalsky's warning was ignored.

CHAPTER 14

As Hattie settled in the back of the limousine she absently hummed "I'm on the Battlefield for My Lord." She was feeling good about today. It was as though she didn't have a care in the world, but the same couldn't be said about her friends.

"Do you think that Larry Smith will change his mind about pressing charges?" Bea asked Josh. She was worried even if Hattie wasn't.

Josh reached over and took Bea's hand. "I think if he was going to do anything he would have come down while Hattie was at the station. I remember reading about him. Over the years there have been a lot of suspicious activities going on at his club. I don't know what his story is, but I'm not surprised that he didn't show up at the police station. He probably wants to stay away from that place."

Connie chuckled, "If I ran a strip club, I wouldn't want people passing out Bibles near my business either. It kind of defeats the purpose."

Everybody laughed. Even Hattie understood the irony of that statement.

When they reached the hotel everyone was exhausted and retired to their rooms. Yet once they were upstairs, Connie toyed with the idea of David and her going out on the town, but he wasn't interested.

"We've been running since we got here so now that we have a little downtime let's stay in for a while. I'll order room service and then I want to talk to you about something."

Connie frowned. She didn't like the sound of this. "Is anything wrong?"

"No, I don't think so," he answered unconvincingly. "We just need to talk."

When room service arrived they had the waiter set up their dinner on the balcony. David had ordered two lobster and steak dinners with all of the trimmings, complete with a waiter to serve it. Romantic music drifted out onto the patio from the room's entertainment center. Connie was impressed.

"This is much better than going out for another night on the town."

After they were finished eating and the remnants of the meal had been taken away, they relaxed on the balcony with a bottle of champagne.

"Everything was lovely David." She gave him a soft smile which he returned.

Sipping their drinks, they sat in silence enjoying each other's company. Their relationship was a strong one. Comfortable silences between them were not uncommon, but Connie was growing a bit anxious about what David had to say to her.

Finally, he cleared his throat. "I know you and your friends have discussed us—me—and I was wondering what's the verdict?"

Connie feigned indignation. "My, my, don't you have a big ego. Why would we discuss you?"

"Because I know women talk. I'm serious, Connie. You seem comfortable with me around them so I'm curious about what they think about our relationship?"

Connie could see that this really was important to him. She was touched.

"Everyone likes you, Hon. They see what I see in you—kindness, consideration. Hattie has really taken to you."

David laughed. "She's something else. I admire her dedication to her cause."

His mood grew serious. "So does this mean that our age difference no longer matters to you? Are you still hesitant?"

Connie's heart began to race. Oh Lord, not the marriage question again. She gave a weary sigh.

"David, I don't hesitate because of what my friends or anyone else thinks. I just know that marriage is a solid commitment, and I've been there and done that."

Connie caressed his face lovingly. "We've talked about this before. You've never been married and at some point you might regret not marrying someone younger who is willing to have children."

David looked at her steadily. "You're not talking to some young blood, Connie. At this stage in my life I know what I want. Besides, I'm not asking you to marry me."

Surprised, Connie blinked. David gave a wry smile.

"Don't get me wrong. I love you and some day I'd like to make us legal, but there's a saying that goes something like if you love something let it go and if it was yours it will return to you."

Connie's eyes narrowed. "So what are you saying? You're letting me go?"

"Hell no!" David chuckled. "You can't get rid of me that easily. What I'm telling you is that they'll be no more pressure. When and if you're ever ready for legalities, let me know. Until then, I'm yours for as long as you want."

Dumbfounded, Connie opened her mouth to speak. David placed a finger to her lips.

"Don't say a thing. Just know that I love you, Constance Palmer and that I'm here for you." He sealed that promise with a long, slow, passionate kiss that left her breathless.

****

After resting a while following the giveaway, Bea and Josh decided to go out later that evening. As they stood outside of a luxury hotel waiting on the valet to bring their rental car, they critiqued the glitzy theatrical production that they had just seen.

"That was absolutely breath-taking!" Bea exclaimed. "But I can't believe how I behaved in there."

Josh pulled her to him. "I don't think that you were the only one crying when the father died." He paused and then teased, "Of course I didn't see anybody else boo-hooing."

"Oh be quiet." She swatted at him playfully and he ducked. Chuckling at their antics, Bea hooked her arm through his and sighed contentedly. There were a lot of good things that she would remember about being in Las Vegas, but being with Josh was at the top of the list.

His rental car came and he helped her into it. They cruised down a crowded boulevard until Joshua turned onto the interstate. After a rather long ride, he exited onto a quiet two lane road and then came to a stop near a small lake.

"Your habit of driving down dark secluded roads is starting to worry me," Bea chided as she remembered a similar escapade in Indianapolis.

"Actually, you're referring to my habit of wanting you all to myself," he corrected.

Parking the car, he walked around to open her door. They strolled to the front of the car where he lifted her onto the hood. Bea gasped, surprised and impressed that he was able to do so. She hadn't had anyone do that in a very long time.

Joshua leaned on the hood beside her. "What do you think?" His hand swept the perimeter of their surroundings which was illuminated by the front headlights.

Bea gazed around her. The night was pitch black which made the stars appear to shine brighter. The moon reflected off of the lake creating a shimmering effect, and the night sounds surrounding them seemed magnified. The bright lights of Las Vegas, Nevada twinkling in the distance served as a perfect backdrop for this entire evening. Bea sighed.

"I think that I want us to stay here like this forever."

Josh walked back to the car, reached through the window and turned on the radio. A smooth jazz station was playing. Walking back to Bea, he held out his hand.

"Care to dance?"

Bea smiled at him and looked up at the star filled sky. She felt an overwhelming sense of deja′ vu as her thoughts drifted back to her high school reunion where she had reunited with the love of her life. He had said those very same words to her. But that was then and this was now, and with a different man who was making this moment magical. She slipped her hand into his.

Josh helped her from the car hood and took her into his arms. It was at that moment that she realized that she would always have warm memories of Frank Schaffer, but she had come to terms with his death. Her heart was now free to move on.

****

The jangle of the telephone startled Hattie from her nap. For a moment she was confused by her surroundings. Clearing her head, she answered the phone on the fourth ring. Reverend Trees was on the other end. There was concern in his voice.

"Hattie, are you all right? Vivian called me and told me what happened. I contacted the police station and I was told that you had been released. I've been calling and calling, and leaving messages, but you didn't call me back."

"I'm fine, Samuel." She reassured him. "But it was a good day. I gave the devil a black eye."

The reverend invited her out to dinner, telling her that he had to see for himself that she was okay. She accepted his invitation.

After changing into a flowing yellow sun dress, she combed her hair and gave thanks for how her feathered haircut lay in place without much effort. Nodding approval of her reflection in the mirror, she threw a brightly colored shawl around her shoulders and was ready to meet the reverend downstairs.

Samuel Trees' eyes widened appreciatively when she stepped off the elevator. Hattie picked up on the look. "Is something wrong?" she asked wanting to hear his compliment.

"Yes…well no…I mean," the reverend took a shaky breath. "It's just that I've admired you for so many years as a member of my flock, but I never realized how truly beautiful you are until now." He added hastily. "Not that you weren't beautiful before. You had an inner beauty, but lately I've noticed how attractive you are on the outside too." Realizing that he was putting his foot in his mouth with each word, the poor man stopped talking as he let out a huge sigh. Hattie was enjoying his dilemma. She patted his hand reassuringly. "It's okay Samuel. I guess we both have to get used to the new me."

"What do you say we take a walk before dinner?" He held out his arm to Hattie. She took it and they strolled out into the night.

Having made no decision as to where they would dine ahead of time, they walked until they found a buffet that had come highly recommended in one of the tourist guide books. As they dined, Hattie recounted the entire episode of her Bible giveaway and her experience at the police station with Detective Norwalsky. She gave a dramatic account of how Bea and Connie came to her rescue, and then ended the tale by describing the sea of Sisters of Mercy, dressed in white as they surrounded the jail.

"That old Pharaoh had no choice but to release me from bondage," Hattie declared.

Amused by her colorful Bible reference, Reverend Trees listened attentively and informed her that the police had committed an oversight. A permit had been secured for the give-away. Reverend

Journal, who like himself was unable to attend the event because of convention business, had it in his possession and would see to it that it was presented to the authorities.

"The important thing," he reminded her "is that God protected you and kept you safe when that crowd got rowdy. But this Smith guy seems to really have it in for you. I wonder why?"

"He's a friend of the devil," she answered emphatically. "Plus, he just happens to be the same man who sat beside me on the plane ride here. He boldly admitted to being an atheist—a Godless man!"

The reverend shook his head. "Then I see where he would see you as a threat. Are you sure that there's nothing else?"

"Maybe," Hattie admitted reluctantly. She went on to describe the harrowing plane trip to Vegas. "All I did was announce what seemed obvious to me—that we might be crashing. Then that heathen Smith had the nerve to threaten to sue the airlines. If he was a believer in the first place he wouldn't have been worried about us going down."

"I see." The minister thought it best not to address that statement, so he changed the subject. "I'm sorry that the Bible giveaway wasn't quite the success that you wanted it to be. Maybe we can think of some other ways to distribute the Bibles."

"Oh I haven't given up. God brought me here to accomplish this mission and I intend to do it."

"I have no doubt about that." Reverend Trees added Hattie's tenacity to the growing list of things that he liked about her. "You know, I wasn't looking forward to attending this convention. It's a lot of work and I was exhausted. What I needed was a good vacation. Plus, you and I were just getting to know each other to say nothing about Las Vegas being hotter than Hades this time of the year."

"You're right about that," Hattie laughed.

"But things do work out in God's plan and am I glad about that." He looked at her pointedly and smiled.

After dinner they continued their stroll through the downtown streets. Near Hattie's hotel they stopped to view an amazing laser light show. Hattie hated that the evening had to end. As they entered the lobby of her hotel a desk clerk called out to her.

"Mrs. Collier, there's a message for you here at the front desk."

Hattie threw Reverend Trees a look. "It's probably from Miss Fanny. She's out somewhere gambling. I've told her to stop roaming around Las Vegas throwing good money away. She's probably in some sort of trouble."

"I'm sure she's fine." Reverend Trees reassured her.

It turned out that the message was from Detective Norwalsky. He wanted her to return his call.

Hattie groaned, "I bet that Larry Smith went down to the police station and pressed charges after all."

The reverend patted her arm in support. "Think positive."

Standing in a corner of the lobby, Hattie took out her cell phone and dialed the detective's number. She tried to remain calm.

"Norwalsky here." The detective didn't sound in any better mood than he had been earlier in the day.

"Detective, this is Hattie Collier. You left a message for me to call. Are you about to run me in?"

"Run you in?" Norwalsky didn't try to conceal the amusement in his voice. "Where do you and your friends get this B-movie jargon?"

Hattie bristled. "I'll have you know we don't watch B-movies. Now what is it that you want?"

"I just called to tell you that I did speak to Larry Smith. He's willing to let things go, but he's taken out a restraining order to keep you and your party away from him and his place of business."

Hattie huffed, "Fine. The Bible says to flee the devil and that's exactly what I'll do."

"That's not all." Norwalsky continued. "The city had planned to file charges against you for nearly inciting a riot and for criminal mischief because of that Bible thing."

"You mean the giveaway," Hattie corrected.

"Whatever. Anyway, the department got a tape of your interview from a local television station. We discovered that your words about the giveaway were drowned out by the sound of a horn. We received confirmation that you did not say that you were giving away 10,000 dollars."

"I told you that!" Hattie was still angry that she had been doubted.

"Yes you did," Norwalsky agreed. "It was the news anchor who made the mistake."

"Well I knew that it wasn't me!" Hattie said emphatically and then she added, "Thank you for calling and telling me."

"One more thing," Norwalsky stated.

"What?" Hattie held her breath.

"We found out that someone did secure a permit for the gathering."

"I'm aware of that, and hopefully there will be a refund."

Norwalsky didn't respond to that, but he wasn't finished. "I'd like to know one more thing, Mrs. Collier."

"What's that?"

When will your visit to Las Vegas be over?" His tone was hopeful.

"As a matter of fact we're leaving in a couple of days," she advised.

The detective's sigh of relief was audible. He bid her goodbye and hung up. She shared the good news that had been delivered with the reverend.

"That's great, Hattie!" He was ecstatic. "Now you can enjoy the rest of your stay without that hanging over your head. You know, tomorrow is the last day of the convention. I've been invited to the Journal's home afterward. I'd like you to go with me."

Hattie's eyes lit up. "I'd like that."

They stood in the lobby grinning at each other, resisting the urge to kiss in public. The reverend took Hattie's hand and led her to a bank of elevators. She felt like a giddy school girl as they stood side by side holding hands.

While waiting for a ride upstairs her eyes strayed to an advertising sign that read: FLY HIGH ABOVE VEGAS. The picture showed five Elvis impersonators parachuting from an airplane. One of the jumpers was giving a thumb up. The sign urged its readers to see the real Las Vegas from the sky. Hattie wasn't impressed with the city from the ground or from the air.

"The elevator is here." Reverend Trees' voice interrupted her thoughts. They rode up to her floor. It was there outside of the hotel room door that he finally gave her the kiss that they had both been wanting. It wasn't long, but it was soft and sweet. When they parted Hattie was tingling. All she could do was stand rooted and smile as she watched Samuel back down the hallway sporting a grin as bright as her own. When the elevator doors opened he backed into it his eyes still locked with Hattie's eyes. As the doors closed he wiggled his fingers goodbye. The door closed and he was gone.

Hattie slid her key card in the door and floated into the room. As usual it was empty. Miss Fanny was nowhere to be found, but she didn't care. She wanted to savor the moment that she'd had with Samuel. Today had been one that she would never forget. She had battled the devil and almost won. Plus, she had been kissed by an angel. What more could she want?

Drifting to the window she looked down on the city of multi-colored lights. Sin City was quite some place. It was a hard nut to crack, but it could be done. The Word still needed spreading and there were still Bibles left. All the Lord had to do was show her a way to get them to the people. If only he would send her a sign. And then it happened.

Across the street from the hotel a brightly colored sign blinked off and on: Book a flight to see Las Vegas. The words were similar to the ones that she had read on the sign downstairs. Suddenly it struck her. That was the sign. It was the sign!

Hattie practically shouted. Excited, she wanted to share her revelation with someone, but as she undressed for bed she thought it through and decided that it was best that she kept it to herself. Feelings were still running high after today's effort. It would be better if she went this next route alone. The Lord had shown her the way to spread his word—twice. Now she knew exactly what she should do.

CHAPTER 15

Fanny Collier hadn't had so much fun since she was a young girl. In the last couple of days she had hit most of the hotel casinos on the right side of the Vegas Strip in order to get the free credit that some of them offered to first time gamblers. She was more than prepared to start on the left side of the street in the last few days that remained on the trip. She had been happily surprised at the other enticements that they also offered, such as free drinks and sodas and free entertainment in the lounges. She had taken advantage of them all. As for now, she had decided to spend the morning relaxing in the hotel room, sitting in bed watching television and sipping on a glass of ice tea.

Yes, this was the life. It was hard work going from place to place in the hot Vegas sun trying to get free money. It was true that her luck wasn't holding up as it had when she first arrived. It had been two days since she had won any kind of real money—that is fifty dollars or more. She was beginning to wonder if there wasn't some sort of conspiracy between the hotels against her. But she was a trooper. She was going to keep right on plugging.

Her activities hadn't provided her with the time to keep up with her daughter-in-law and her friends. She knew that Bea and Connie and the men with whom they were involved were all hanging out together. Unlike her daughter-in-law, they would call her daily to see if she was okay and occasionally they would invite her on their sojourns around the city, but she had declined. Four was a double date and five was a crowd. While she appreciated their kindness, she had her own agenda and being a fifth wheel wasn't one of them.

Miss Fanny liked David and Josh. Connie and Bea had been lucky to find such good men. She wished both couples well. Despite Hattie's idiosyncrasies she wanted the same for her with Reverend Trees. He was a fine man and a relationship with him would do her some good. Even though Leon had been her son, she knew that it was time for Hattie to stop holding on to the memory of her late husband. She had been doing so for much too long. It was time for her to move on with her life. All she could hope was that Hattie didn't blow it. She could be way out there some times.

Yesterday, after the Bible giveaway fiasco, Bea and Connie had hauled Hattie back to the hotel room from the police station and called Miss Fanny, filling her in on what had happened. Instead of going to the giveaway with them, Miss Fanny had chosen to troll the casinos. She hadn't been very sympathetic to her daughter-in-law's plight regarding the results of her stunt. It was her fear that Hattie's activities could interfere with the free money that she was getting from the hotels if it became known that she was related to the nutcase. After all they did have the same last name, and her daughter-in-law's escapades had been scattered across the media. She didn't have a problem with Hattie battling sin in Vegas any other time, but why did she have to do it when her mother-in-law was on a roll? So when Miss Fanny had arrived at the room last night, she found Hattie there and told her to cool it. That had been the wrong thing to say.

Hattie had gotten snippy and started telling Miss Fanny about herself and her weakness as a Christian. It was on then.

Miss Fanny called Hattie a Holier than thou heifer. Hattie countered by telling her that she was a hypocrite who served the Lord in Indianapolis and the devil in Las Vegas. Miss Fanny informed her that the blinking Jesus earrings made her look like a fool, while Hattie insisted that the fool was running around Vegas trying to gyp casinos out of five bucks each. It got so heated that when David and Joshua came to the room to invite Miss Fanny to accompany them on a midnight jaunt to the casino, they had to separate the two women whose verbal sparring was growing intense. The men took Miss Fanny downstairs to gamble, and called Bea and Connie to comfort Hattie who was so upset that she held a prayer session for Miss Fanny's soul since she was positive that the old woman was headed straight to hell.

Miss Fanny had a good time with her two male escorts, even though she lost money in the slot machine. As for Hattie, Miss Fanny had decided that she was in her own world. She wasn't sure that the woman was even operating with a full deck.

Hattie had been asleep when Miss Fanny returned to the room later, and when she awoke this morning Hattie had already gone out. It was mid afternoon when the talk show that she had been watching ended and Miss Fanny figured that it was time to get ready to hit the Strip.

She quickly drained a glass of orange juice and placed the empty glass on the nightstand. She was vaguely aware of the program on the TV set. It was an entertainment news show and the celebrity reporter, Harper Ferry, was giving a live report from Las Vegas. He was standing in front of one of the hotels on the Strip talking about a multi-million dollar deal that some celebrity had struck with one of the hotels. Miss Fanny recognized the spot. She had hit it already and won twenty dollars off her five dollar credit.

Rising from the bed, she had started across the room when Ferry suddenly shouted, "What in the world is that?"

His tone caught Miss Fanny's attention. Peeping back at the screen she saw him looking skyward with a puzzled look on his face.

"Several objects are falling from an airplane buzzing the Strip," he reported. "But I can't quite make them out." He shaded his eyes and squinted. "It looks like small leaflets. Nooo, they're…"

The reporter began screaming. "We're being attacked! We're being bombed! Owww!"

An object hit him squarely in the face. Another one bounced off of the camera lens. The camera tilted upward and the screen went black. The station switched back to the two shocked anchors. It was clear by their expressions that they had been caught off guard. Not prepared to speak without a teleprompter, there were a few seconds of silence as the duo continued to stare straight ahead with stilted smiles plastered on their faces. Two pairs of eyes slide toward one another then back at the camera. Miss Fanny drew closer to the screen and turned up the volume. What was this all about?

Bea was in the upstairs bathroom of their luxurious suite, and Josh was relaxing on the sofa downstairs when he called out to Bea.

"Come quick!"

The urgency in his voice brought her hurrying down the stairs. "What is it?"

He pointed to the television screen. The crawl beneath the broadcast read Harper Ferry – Live from the Las Vegas Strip. On screen the reporter was crouching beneath an awning like a soldier in battle. The camera panned the street to verify his breathless account of the events occurring live on the Strip.

"A few minutes ago a small airplane buzzed over the Las Vegas Strip and started to drop small, but effective weapons down on the heads of the unsuspecting citizens of this great city. People are running for their lives as they duck into buildings, under bus stop benches and into fast food restaurants. Cars, taxis and buses are careening to a halt in a futile effort to avoid the missiles raining from the sky. This reporter is going to put himself in harm's way to trace the source of this mayhem."

Clutching his microphone, Harper did a belly crawl toward the nearest object as he whispered dramatically. "I'm inching my way slowly towards something that could be a compact bomb." He drew closer. "It's square and about six inches in diameter. The color appears to be white with orange… No! It looks like some sort of gold writing." He looked into the camera. "Could it be terrorist propaganda?"

Just at that moment a breeze blew the pages of the object open. Harper screamed, and then back pedaled to the safety of the awning. Off camera the cameraman could be heard saying, "For god sakes, Harper, it's just a book."

The reporter looked into the camera. "As a former war correspondent, I've learned that nothing can be taken for granted." He reached out and quickly grabbed the object then read the words on the front. "Holy Bible?"

Bea's eyes widened. "A Bible?"

Harper's eyes narrowed as he appeared to forget that he was on camera, "You mean I was hit in the face with a damn Bible? This thing could have put my freaking eye out!"

"Psst! Psst! Harper we're still live," the cameraman frantically reminded him.

Regaining his composure, Harper smiled fetchingly into the camera. "It's a Bible, ladies and gentlemen, a small white leather book with the words Holy Bible written in raised gold lettering." He held it up for everyone to see.

"Oh my God!" Bea groaned as she recognized the evidence. "Hattie, what have you done?"

"When I think that someone has defiled the sacred word—" His voice cracked as he got teary eyed. "Just give me a moment." Taking a handkerchief from his pocket he dabbed at his eyes. "You can be assured that Info Hollywood will launch a full investigation to find out who is responsible for this diabolical act."

Sitting in her hotel room mesmerized by what she was seeing on the TV screen, Connie was muttering, "I don't believe this. I just don't believe this."

One of the anchors observed gravely, "Thank you, Harper. We'll get back to you as we get more details on this breaking news story. Be safe out there. " The anchor brightened. "In other news tonight—"

Miss Fanny hit the TV set off button and turned her cell phone up. She knew her daughter-in-law's work when she saw it.

"Here we go again." She grumbled as she prepared for the telephone calls that she knew would be coming from Hattie's friends. The cops would probably throw Hattie's loony tune butt under the jail this time, and from what she had just seen, her daughter-in-law probably deserved it.

CHAPTER 16

During the next 24 hours Hattie, Bea, Connie and Miss Fanny learned from firsthand experience the meaning of the words media circus. It started with the noon news the day that Hattie decided to bombard the Las Vegas Strip with Bibles. Every channel in Las Vegas made her antics its lead story. The landing of the plane that she had used to do the deed and her arrest were broadcast live. By the time the day progressed an array of pseudo news, talk and entertainment shows had elevated her actions to mythic proportions.

Info Hollywood opened with dramatic music played over colorful graphics that spelled out the title of the program in bright red: The Bible Bomber: An American Dilemma. A solemn looking Harper Ferry looked into the camera.

"Hello ladies and gentlemen, and welcome to an Info Hollywood Investigative Report Special. I'm Harper Ferry and I'm standing in front of City Hall where the Las Vegas Police Department, known as the Metro, has taken alleged Bible Bomber, Hattie Collier in for questioning. As the world knows by now Mrs. Collier—who is suspected of being connected to the neo-conservative right—was arrested at a small airport outside of Las Vegas as the mastermind of the bombing of the famed Strip. Arrested as an accomplice was Paul Archer, the pilot of the small plane used to rain Bibles on the unsuspecting heads of innocent citizens, including, yours truly. I was nearly blinded in the attack. The devastating extent of my possible career-ending injury is as yet unknown."

He pointed to a cut above his eyebrow. "Can you pan in on this?" he asked the cameraman. After several failed attempts to find the tiny cut, the frustrated cameraman pulled back into a medium shot of Ferry urging him to "keep going". The reporter complied.

"Authorities wouldn't comment on Mrs. Collier's assault on this city as they led her and the pilot of the plane to the squad cars, but while the authorities might have remained mum on the subject, Mrs. Collier had plenty to say—or shall I say sing, as did the pilot."

The camera cut to Hattie, surrounded by uniformed officers. With her head held high, she was clutching a Bible to her bosom and singing, "I'm on the Battlefield for My Lord," at the top of her lungs. Meanwhile, other officers were dragging the pilot—a lanky, bearded, unkempt man wearing a dirty baseball cap and a camouflage jacket—to another squad car as he loudly protested his innocence.

"I don't know nothing about nothing! She hired me to fly over the Strip and drop pamphlets! That's all she paid me for! I just thought they was real thick pamphlets. There was so many they almost brought my plane down with the weight. I just tossed 'em; I didn't read 'em."

The camera cut back to Harper Ferry who is caught smoothing his eyebrows. He jumped when made aware of the camera and looked grim.

"The background of this strange story begins in Hattie Collier's hometown, Indianapolis, Indiana, where we'll find fellow correspondent Hiawatha Jones."

The camera cut to a close up shot of a blond, blue eyed female correspondent with a toothpaste ad smile.

"Thank you, Harper." The smile was instantly replaced by a serious demeanor. "I'm here live in Indianapolis, where race cars and a Super Bowl winning football team rule. It is a conservative community filled with God fearing, church going people who love their Bibles." Hiawatha held up a white, leather bound Bible. "Behind me is the home of Hattie Collier, the Bible Bomber."

Over the reporter's shoulder the camera did a long shot of the exterior of Hattie's house as Hiawatha continued speaking.

"It is a modest dwelling where Mrs. Collier, a widow in her sixties, lives with her mother-in-law, Mrs. Fanny Collier. Info Hollywood tried to speak with the mother-in-law in Las Vegas, but she was not receptive."

There was a shot of Miss Fanny heading toward the elevator in her hotel. The reporter tried to stick a microphone in front her face and Miss Fanny knocked it out of her hand, and then began hitting the woman with her purse. A series of bleeps replaced what Miss Fanny said to the woman as she beat her. The camera cut back to Hiawatha.

"As you can see, she had little to say. However, their next door neighbor, Miss Peaches Perkins, describes the Bible Bomber as "good people."

Peaches Perkins a tall, willowy woman in her twenties stepped into the camera shot. Her makeup was moderate, but her shoulder length bob was tinted at the ends with blue and as she spoke she looked directly into the camera, ignoring the reporter.

"Miss Hattie has lived in this neighborhood for over thirty years. I've known that woman all of my life. My mother and her are friends. Miss Hattie is good people." Peaches brushed her fingers through her hair as she primped for the camera. "Of course she was a little nosey now and then, always in my business, talkin' to my mama about how she needs to make me pay rent and everything." She stops short as she catches herself venting. She flashed a smile, highlighted by a gold tooth. "I'm a beautician, you know. I freelance, Perms by Peaches."

Suddenly, she ripped her blouse open and buttons flew about haphazardly. One of them hit Hiawatha in her forehead. The reporter uttered a shriek of pain, as Peaches reveals a t-shirt underneath her blouse. Printed across the front of it are the words Perms by Peaches along with the telephone number. Realizing that the show is being used for promotional purposes Hiawatha quickly recovers and intervenes.

"Thank you, Miss Perkins."

Holding her injured head, Hiawatha tried to elbow the young woman out of the way. Instead, Peaches boldly steps in front of Hiawatha and turns her back to the camera, gesturing to the ad which is also printed on the back of the t-shirt in iridescent red, followed by the words call me.

An irritated Hiawatha tries to step in front of Peaches again and a shoving match begins between the two women as Peaches whirls on the reporter.

"Who you pushing, bit…?"

Peaches last words are bleeped as the camera quickly cuts back to Harper. For a moment he stands looking unprepared, but he hastily recovers.

"Uh, we have another report from Indianapolis where Mrs. Collier, the grandmother of four, is a long time member of a church that reportedly she helped found. Rusty Pinn, are you there?"

The camera cuts to a tall, handsome young black man dressed impeccably in a stylish suit.

"Yes I am, Harper, and I tried earlier to interview Hattie Collier's two adult children, but they have gone into seclusion. But as you've pointed out, I am here at the Lord of Mercy Missionary Baptist church where Mrs. Collier is one of the founding members. Here with me are two of her friends and fellow parishioners, Dorothy Riggs and Thelma Reeves."

He turned to the two ladies standing side by side, dressed in their Sunday best complete with large church hats. Both women are clutching Bibles. He put the mike in Thelma's face first.

"Mrs. Reeves, how long have you known Mrs. Collier?"

Looking stiff and nervous, Thelma barely spoke above a whisper. "I have known Hattie Collier since high school. Her father, God rest his soul, was a minister and my family went to his church."

Dorothy displays no shyness in front of the camera and tries unsuccessfully to grab the mike from Rusty as she speaks. "My family was in his church too. We all went to Crispus Attacks High School together, and all of us were in each other's weddings. Hattie Collier is a God fearing woman…"

"A religious fanatic?" Rusty interrupted.

Ignoring him, Dorothy continues to speak. "And when her father died and a man of the devil took over her Daddy's church, Hattie and her husband, Leon followed Thelma's husband…"

"The late Reverend Theofus J. Reeves," Thelma interjected.

"And they helped all of us found the Lord of Mercy…"

Rusty jumps on this new information. "So you are all involved in religious conservatism?"

"We are involved in spreading the word of the Lord!" Dorothy countered.

"Yes!" Thelma agreed with a shake of her head. The hat she is wearing nearly takes Rusty's eye out as he jumps back. Dorothy takes advantage of his temporary distraction.

"We are foot soldiers in the army of the Lord and it is our duty to save souls."

"Amen!" Thelma shouted.

Rusty raised a brow. "Then do I hear you saying that you're religious militants?"

"Whenever and wherever we find sin, we fight it," said Dorothy. "And Hattie found plenty of it in Las Vegas."

"Preach!" Thelma started waving her hands in the air and getting happy

"She's a heroine, not a hellion," Dorothy declared.

"Amen! Amen!" Thelma started to jump up and down in place.

"And this," Dorothy held the Bible up to the camera, "is a heroine's weapon!"

"Praise Jesus!" Thelma goes into a full shout with Dorothy joining her as the Bible waving duo gave praise. Startled by the religious fervor, Rusty addresses the camera.

"There you have it, Harper. Bible Bomber, Hattie Collier, is she a religious zealot or a religious heroine?"

Later that day on the radio program, The Talk and Talk Some More Show, there was another spin taken. Ultra conservative host, Husky Lambert asked his listening audience: Is the Bible Bomber a Religious Zealot or a Liberal Puppet? His telephone lines were jammed with listeners who were certain that they knew the answer. Among those who called in was a voice that was familiar to Hattie and her friends.

"I have Charmaine Shaffer on the line," said Lambert, "She's calling from…" He hesitated. "Uh, the state Women's Correctional Prison in Rockville, Indiana." He cleared his throat. "She says that she knows Hattie Collier, personally. Even more important is that she says that she can prove that Collier's so-called religious zeal is a cover for ultra liberal leanings. Mrs. Shaffer?"

Charmaine's voice was strident. "Yes, I've known Hattie Collier and her gang of lying gossip mongers since high school and over the years they have all engaged in supporting Communists-leaning activities."

"Communists?" Lambert perked up. "You mean they're spies? I suspected that they might have Socialists leanings; but you say they're Communists?"

"Most certainly—Communist, Socialists—does it matter? They are just wrong." Her voice dripped with distain. "They have engaged in posing as police officers to gather intelligence…"

"About the government?" Lambert sounded incredulous.

“Well, one of Hattie’s best friends, Bea Belle, she worked high up in government in the state capital.”

“Oh my God!’ Lambert groaned. “Who knows what secrets that she shared with those godless enemies of the State!”

“Speaking of God, Hattie belongs to some church that she and her followers started. I doubt if it’s even legitimate. I believe its some kind of cult. Plus, she’s started some sort of funeral business that extorts money from grieving relatives to throw parties for the deceased.”

Lambert slammed a fist on the desk in front of him, “Ladies and gentlemen if that’s not proof of how these liberals cuddle this country’s enemies, then I don’t know what is! This lady is saying that the Bible Bomber is a liberal and a Communist. I don’t know what to make of it except to say these people don’t care who they exploit or how they do it”

“Who knows what kind of propaganda was inside of those Bibles!” Charlie Mae had made a believer out of Lambert about her conspiracy theory and she wasn’t going to let him go.

“No good Christian is going to treat the Bible like that! Decent citizens should demand an investigation of her activities.”

Worked into a frenzy, Lambert agreed. “Bible loving Christians everywhere we need to bombard the Las Vegas authorities with the demand that they reveal every single word of the messages concealed inside of those defaced Bibles.”

It didn’t take long after that broadcast for the phone lines in Vegas to light up.

On the late night television news show, The Night Light, a debate raged. Members of The Psychological Impact of Theology and the members of Animals are People Endangered engaged in a heated exchange.

“How many cows must die to satisfy the lust for the leather used on the cover of Bibles?” The A.P.E. representative cried emotionally.

“Who cares!” hollered the P.I.T. pundit. “Cows don’t have souls.”

The physical brawl that resulted made the morning newspapers. However, the headline read: Bible Bomber Causes Debate Uproar! Can Anybody Save Las Vegas?

****

Connie tossed the morning newspaper aside with a groan. Bea turned the morning news show off with an even bigger one. Everyone was gathered in Josh's suite trying to avoid the press and comfort each other. Miss Fanny was sitting on the sofa with her head in her hand looking glum. She summed up the thoughts of everyone present.

"What in the world has Hattie gotten herself into?"

At that moment her telephone rang. Checking the i.d., she let it ring.

"Aren't you going to answer it?" Bea asked half-heartedly. All of their telephones, both cells and hotel phones had been ringing off of the hooks since yesterday.

"No," answered Miss Fanny. "It's just my grandchildren wanting to holler at me again about their mother. What am I suppose to tell them, that the woman is crazy? They should know that by now."

"I just don't understand why Hattie refuses to accept bail?" Bea lamented. "What is she trying to prove?"

"That she's right," Miss Fanny was certain about that. If she had her daughter-in-law here with her right now, she would strangle her with her bare hands. The woman's insanity was interrupting her gambling.

"Well she's started a mess that's getting deeper and deeper," said Connie, who was behind the bar mixing herself a badly needed drink. "I still can't believe that Charlie Mae had the nerve to call a radio station from behind bars. I thought there were laws about that sort of thing."

"She just wanted to stir up more trouble." Bea was so angry when she heard about that call that she wanted to fly back to Indianapolis and kick her butt. This time it was her cell phone that rang. Simultaneously, Joshua came bounding down the staircase with his cell phone clinging to his ear.

He joined the others in the living room while Bea answered her telephone. David waited patiently for Josh to indicate that his call was over before addressing him. Joshua had been calling friends of his around town to find out what could be done to help Hattie. He disconnected his call.

"What have you found out?" asked David.

"Councilman Summers said that the mayor is up in arms. It seems that since yesterday attendance on the Strip has taken a nose dive. The casino owners are giving him a fit. It looks like Hattie's going to have to pay for tossing those Bibles." He sat down beside Bea who had disconnected her call.

"Reverend Trees is on his way up. He thinks that he can get through the press without being noticed. I told him that they don't know about this hotel suite so make sure none of them follow him."

"Good," Miss Fanny grunted. "If another reporter sticks a microphone in my face I'm going to put him in the hospital."

"You are deadly with that purse, Miss Fanny," David chuckled.

"And it was full of change too." She grinned proudly.

There was a knock on the door. Bea went to answer it. She peeked through the eye hole. On the other side was a man dressed in maintenance overalls.

"Yes?" Bea frowned, wondering who had sent for him. Nothing was wrong in Josh's suite as far as she knew.

"It's me," the man whispered clandestinely and looked up. "Reverend Trees."

Still uncertain, Bea put the chain on the door and cracked it for a better look. Recognizing him, she opened the door and he slipped into the room like a thief in the night. He looked pleased with himself.

"Were you followed?" She doubled locked the door.

"No, I wasn't." The reverend acknowledged everyone's greeting. "And I've got news about Hattie."

The chorus of "whats" echoed through the room. He took a seat in the only empty chair in the room before speaking.

"We plan on getting her out of there." There was resolve in the reverend's words. "The ministers at the conference have put a call out for Sisters of Mercy within 500 miles to come into the city and demonstrate for Hattie's right to spread the Word. I left the convention center an hour ago and they are coming in by the bus loads. They plan on demonstrating in front of City Hall in nonviolent protest, like they did during the Civil Rights Movement, until Hattie is freed."

He looked at everyone in the room with a sense of satisfaction, expecting an excited reaction. Nobody looked thrilled.

"What?" He didn't understand the lack of enthusiasm.

"Well, I guess that they will be joining the APES, protesting the use of leather on Bibles," said Miss Fanny.

"And the PITS who will be conducting a pro-religion demonstration," added Bea.

"To say nothing of the Atheist Against the Spread of Seminaries," Connie piped in.

"And the SLUGSS," David reminded everyone.

He observed Connie's questioning look. "The Simply Living Up To God's Standards Society," he explained. "That's Lambert's group. According to the latest news reports, who knows how many more groups have vowed to rally in front of City Hall tomorrow."

"It looks like Las Vegas is really about to light up," Miss Fanny concluded. She added dryly, "I can hardly wait."

CHAPTER 17

Reliving the scene of her arrest, Hattie blinked back tears of humiliation as she stood in a drab Las Vegas jail cell. As the Bible drop was being made, she had been waiting patiently inside a hanger at the small Las Vegas Airport from which the plane had been launched. When she heard the plane's engine signaling its return, she hurried outside and was surprised to see the parade of police cruisers arrive at the landing strip with sirens wailing. Her curiosity had mounted as the cars screeched to a stop and police officers poured out of their vehicles, guns drawn. She had looked around nervously wondering if some mass murderer had escaped and targeted the airport as a hideout. Since she had paid the pilot for his services and he took off with her cargo, Hattie hadn't seen another soul out in this desolate area. If so, she would have noticed.

A feeling of anxiety had replaced her curiosity as she watched the plane roll to a stop and a small army of officers descended on the single engine aircraft that had "Fly High" blazoned across its sides. With their guns drawn, the authorities had watched the propellers slow to a stop. All eyes had been locked on the plane's cabin door as it slowly creaked open.

Paul Archer, the lanky framed pilot, appeared in the plane's doorway. Shakily, he tried to step out of the plane, but his unsteady steps turned into a combination jump/fall to the ground. He landed with a complaining "Hump!"

As he stood, he ran his hands over his body as if checking for broken bones. It wasn't until he straightened to his full five feet ten inches and stretched with his arms high in the air that he noticed the police officers. Frozen in that position, he stopped, blinked and slowly turned in a circle observing all of the guns pointed straight at him.

"Whatever it is, I didn't do it," he had declared loudly.

The officer-in-charge signaled two of his men to either side of the inebriated pilot. They forced his arms behind his back. Deftly they handcuffed him as the officer-in-charge asked, "What is your name, sir?"

"Paul Archer." The pilot weaved unsteadily on his feet as he tried to show some dignity.

"What's this about?"

"Paul Archer," the officer declared, "you are under arrest for assault, criminal negligence and endangerment." He read him his rights.

Archer's only response to that was a loud, toxic belch. Assailed by the stench, the men closest to him took an involuntary step back.

By this time Hattie had rushed from her vantage point outside the hanger to the commotion on the landing strip. An officer stopped her advance as she tried to push her way into the center of the circle.

"Why are you arresting this man?" She hollered to no one in particular, not sure where she should settle her angry glare. Her question caught the attention of the man in charge.

"Who are you madam? " He nodded for the other officer to let her come forward.

"I'm Mrs. Hattie Collier," she responded haughtily as she went to face him.

"Do you know this man or anything about his activities?" he demanded in a no nonsense tone.

"Mr. Archer is helping me do the Lord's work."

"No," the officer-in-charge corrected, "this man is breaking the law."

"Hattie's eyes widened. "How do you figure that?"

"Are you aware that he dropped books from his plane down on the heads of innocent people? He's lucky he didn't kill somebody."

"Books!" Hattie was appalled by his description. "Those weren't just books. Those were Bibles."

The officer snatched his mirrored sunglasses from his eyes, "Madame, those were weapons."

Hattie bristled. "The word of the Lord is what this town needs. Bibles don't hurt they heal!"

"Bibles?" Paul Archer continued to weave unsteadily as he monitored the exchange. "What Bibles? What is she talking about? All I did was drop them pamphlets on the Strip."

Hattie caught a whiff of his breath. "Mr. Archer, are you drunk?"

Archer straightened his shoulders and said proudly, "Yes I am."

"Oh, Lord." Hattie was distressed. "You weren't drunk before you went up!"

"No I wasn't," Archer agreed. "It's the clouds, Madame. They do something to me."

The officer-in-charge glanced disapprovingly at the man then turned his attention back to Hattie. "And you say that this man was helping you do the Lord's work?" He raised a questioning brow. "Now, what exactly is your role in this?"

Insisting that Paul Archer had been sober when he went up in the air, Hattie began to explain about the Bibles and her idea for making sure that the residents and visitors in Las Vegas received the Word.

The officer-in charge snapped his fingers as he eyed Hattie with greater scrutiny. "You're the lady mixed up in that $10,000 give-away scam." He motioned to another officer. "We're taking her in too."

Hattie drew away indignantly as the officer grabbed her elbow. "I was not part of any scam! I didn't do a thing!"

"Except pay me," Archer offered as he was led away.

"And now she's going to jail," the officer snapped. Turning, he marched back to his squad car.

When Hattie and the pilot arrived at the police station she had been searched, finger printed and a mug shot had been taken. She recoiled at the idea that she had been thrown into this hell hole like some criminal. Maybe it wasn't the filthy, urine-smelling, tin-cup-banging-against-the bars kind of place she had imagined, but it was still jail! She learned from one of the other women locked up with her that she was being held in what was called a holding cell and that she and most of the others in there with her were waiting on a bond hearing. She would need bail money! For a moment Hattie had been in a panic. What would her children and grandchildren say? Could her friends come up with the money to get her out of here?

Then suddenly, calm returned. Hattie squared her shoulders. She had done the Lord's work and she was being persecuted. She made a pact with herself that she would stay in jail until her trial. Why should her friends and family have to sacrifice for her? The Lord would see her through.

Satisfied with that decision, she turned her attention to the other women in the cell. There were approximately fifteen of them of all ages. Hattie appeared to be the oldest of the group. As she edged along the wall observing the others, she realized that there was no place to sit. The chairs were all occupied as were the few cots that were available. A plump blonde woman standing beside one of the cots watched Hattie as she moved around the cell. Suddenly, without warning, the blonde slapped one of the women sitting on a cot.

"Get up and let grandma have a sit," she barked.

The thin-as-a-rail victim leaped up, fist balled, ready to do battle. "You shouldn't have done that!"

"I'm tired of having to tell you everything," the blonde growled.

She seemed fearless and in charge, although she was much shorter than the woman confronting her. Observing the two, Hattie thought of a cartoon her children watched when they were young. It featured two dogs, one a small terrier and the other a burley bull dog. The small dog was a tough talker and the bigger dog was constantly trying to please him. The two women were so similar to those cartoon characters that Hattie nearly laughed aloud.

"Ladies," she intervened, "there's no reason to fight. I can stand up. Or better yet, why don't we take turns sitting down since there doesn't seem to be enough seating."

"Whatever," the blonde sniffed. "By the way, I'm Janet and this is my partner, Renee."

After the introductions, Janet confided that the two of them had been arrested for petty theft.

"Renee screwed up." Janet paused to roll her eyes at her friend. "The woman who said we was trying to steal from her turned out to be an undercover cop. So what you in for?" she inquired.

Before Hattie could respond, a commotion in the corridor drew everyone's attention. The jailers were dragging a young woman down the hall as she screamed obscenities at her captors. Once the holding cell door was opened, she was unceremoniously pushed inside the cell.

Hattie stared in open- mouth astonishment as the woman, who looked to be no older than twenty years old, continued her profanity laced tirade oblivious to the fact that the officers were ignoring her. When she finally ran out of steam, she turned to her fellow cell mates.

"So what are you looking at?" She demanded before stomping over to a wall and sliding down on the floor.

Hattie noted the girl's hot pink shorts. They were so tight that she wondered why they hadn't ripped when she sat down. They certainly exposed enough butt cheeks. The matching pink halter top that she wore barely covered her ample bosom. Completing the outfit was a pair of long white plastic boots. Hattie hadn't seen a pair of those in years.

The majority of the other women paid her little attention, but Hattie was both fascinated and heartbroken as she watched the sulking young woman. It was obvious that she was practicing the world's oldest profession, but this was someone's daughter living here in this vulgar city selling her body. She was to be pitied . Hattie approached her.

"Sweetheart?"

The girl ignored her. Hattie tried again.

"Sweetheart, what is your name?"

The girl looked up at her and snarled, "What's it to you?"

Hattie wouldn't be dissuaded.

She wasn't sure why this particular young woman touched her, maybe it was because she had a daughter and but for the grace of God this could have been her child when she was younger. It made her wonder how someone this young got so morally twisted. She had to ask.

"Honey, where are your parents? Do they know you're out here like this?"

The girl snickered. "Do yours? Ain't you a little old to be out here trickin'?"

The older woman frowned in confusion. "Trickin'?"

Janet spoke up "She thinks you turn tricks. You know—" Janet made a circle with her fingers and ran a finger in and out of it.

Hattie still looked confused. Janet bent down and whispered in her ear. Hattie drew back in horror.

"Sweet Jesus! I never heard such filth in my life. I certainly am not doing any tricks! What is your name?"

"Lola" she answered with a sardonic smile.

Janet took over. She leveled the young woman with a don't-mess-with- me look. "So Lola, Grandma asked you your name and I don't believe she meant your street name. So what is it?"

'Lola' sized up the menacing blond and noticed the taller woman standing close behind her. She turned back to Hattie. "My real name is Christina Hall."

"Nice to meet you, Christina." Hattie smiled warmly at the honey-colored girl with the big brown eyes. She was pretty, but could be beautiful without all of the makeup she was wearing. "So, do your parents know what you're doing?"

Christina sighed loudly. "You sound like you're my friggin' mother. Ain't nothing wrong with what I do. I support myself and I don't hurt nobody."

Hattie disagreed. "Your family will be hurt if they find out what you do. What example are you setting for other girls? And if the men you're with are married, what about their wives?"

"What's with you?" Christina was becoming irritated by the conversation. "It's my body and I can do what I want. And if the women took care of business, their husbands wouldn't be with me no way. Anyway, the difference between me and a lot of girls who's suppose to be dating some man is that I get paid. I can make more money in one night than I could in two weeks workin' at some burger joint. I'm not on welfare or looking for a handout so what's with the self-righteous crap?"

Hattie looked into Christina's eyes. She didn't know her story but she was sure that she could see fear in then in spite of her bravado.

"What about your health? What about your soul?" She asked softly. "God has a better plan for your life. Whatever happened to get you on these streets can be fixed by Him if you'd only ask."

"Oh yeah?" Christina chuckled. "Then what did he put you in here for?"

Hattie hesitated. Why was she in here?

"Well, I don't actually know what the legal crime was, but I know that I was doing the Lord's work and not the devil's. I had a plan for every person in Las Vegas to have access to God's word. All I did was arrange for a few Bibles to be dropped from an airplane onto that godless Las Vegas strip," Hattie said proudly.

Her declaration was met with murmured comments and laughter from the other women in the cell.

"That's hilarious."

"That's the lamest story I ever heard."

"I'm going to try that one on the judge."

"Vegas sure got some tough littering laws."

Christina wiped tears of laughter from her eyes. "You're good, lady. For a second I thought you were seriously trying to preach to me but you were just jerking me around."

"I was not!" Hattie didn't let the taunts discourage her. "What I said was true. I didn't think that I was committing a crime. I was spreading the word of God."

Christina looked at her balefully, "I don't think that I'm committing a crime either. I'm just spreading a little joy and making money in the process."

"Hattie Collier."

Hattie jumped at the sound of her name being bellowed out in the corridor. A police officer stopped in front of the cell. Peering between the bars, he called her name again.

Hattie indicated her presence. "I'm Hattie Collier."

"Let's go. It's time to go before the judge."

As Hattie moved toward the door, she stopped and turned back to Christina.

"No matter what we do, child, God is always willing to forgive. When you leave here find a church, talk to a minister, get help. You are too young to waste any more of your time here on earth."

To Christina's surprise, Hattie hugged her.

"Collier!" The police officer called out impatiently.

Hattie exited the jail cell, but as the door closed behind her she turned back one last time.

"Trust in the Lord, Christina." Hattie advised.

The message was ignored, but it didn't matter. As Hattie walked away from the holding cell her resolve was absolute. She had done the right thing spreading the word of the Lord in this cesspool of sin. Nobody was going to tell her any different, not even some judge.

CHAPTER 18

"She did what?"

Bea withdrew the telephone from her ear as Michael Collier's voice reverberated across the room. Connie and she were sitting in the confines of the building that housed the headquarters of the Las Vegas Police Department. Quietly, Bea repeated what she had just said to Hattie's son.

"Your mother refused bail. She told the judge that in protest of the sin and corruption that runs throughout Las Vegas, she was going to stay in jail."

Michael groaned dejectedly as his sister, Cynthia, who was on the other end of the three-way call picked up the slack.

"Where's grandma? Maybe she can talk Mama into accepting bail."

Bea almost imitated Michael's groan. How could she tell the two of them that Miss Fanny was back on the Strip gambling? After Hattie had taken her stand before the judge, Miss Fanny had taken a stance as well.

"Let the fool stay in jail," she had declared. Then she had announced to Bea and Connie that she was going "sinning" on the Strip. "And I better not get hit in the head with no Bibles!"

The last time that Bea had seen the woman she was leaving the building by the back stairs to avoid the media. That had been hours ago and they hadn't heard from her since. There was no way that she could tell that to Hattie's children. Instead Bea chose to be ambiguous.

"She's not available right now."

"Where is she?" Cynthia had always been nosey.

"She's in the bathroom," Bea lied.

"What's going to happen to Mama?" Hattie's daughter whined.

That was another thing about Hattie's youngest child that had always irked Bea. Even when she was a little girl coming to Bea's house to play she whined about everything.

"According to the bailiff that we talked to they were going to put her back into the holding cell. We're here in the police station now waiting to see her. We're all scheduled to leave here tomorrow and we're hoping that we won't have to leave without her." Bea didn't tell them that Miss Fanny had advised them to do just that.

"I'm tired of Hattie's better than thou attitude," the older woman had snorted. "Sometime a little bit of sin can be fun."

Bea couldn't disagree and she understood Miss Fanny's position, but it was difficult thinking about abandoning Hattie. The two of them had been friends forever. If their situations had been reversed, she knew that Hattie would have been right there by her side. But, enough was enough!

It was true that she wasn't turning cartwheels about Hattie's stubborn antics, and it wasn't because she was for or against her friend's cause like so many of those idiots demonstrating outside. Her resentment of this whole affair was personal. Hattie's foolishness was interfering with Bea's relationship with Josh, the man who had shown no hesitation in helping her friend, not only with purchasing Bibles, but he had helped her retain an attorney. He had gone beyond the call of duty when it came to helping Hattie and had asked for nothing in return.

As Michael and Cynthia babbled on, Bea pretended to listen while her mind drifted back to last night after everyone had left Josh's suite. The two of them had been alone and he had folded her in his arms and held her close.

"Don't worry," he had whispered against her hair. "Everything will be okay,"

She had felt comforted by his words. He had tightened his hold on her and they could have stood like that forever as far as she was concerned. She had raised her head and looked into his eyes. Slowly, Josh had lowered his head as she raised her lips to his and they had kissed passionately. It had been glorious. It hadn't been like the other kisses that they had shared. This one was different. It had been filled with urgency, a purpose, an unfulfilled wanting and need that neither of them had expressed in words.

Over the months as they were getting to know one another Josh had been a patient man, an absolute gentleman, never pushing her, never asking for more than she was willing to give. Bea wanted him as much as that kiss told her that he wanted her. She wanted to fulfill both of their sexual desires, but she wasn't of the generation where making that decision was easy as it seemed to be these days.

As the kiss had deepened and both of their hands had begun to roam, need had spiraled and threatened to get out of control. Articles of clothing were disheveled and discarded when the phone rang and there was a knock on the door at the same time. Preoccupied, they had been oblivious to both, but the ringing and knocking persisted. Frustrated, Josh had stormed to the door and shouted to whoever was on the other side that they were busy. Bea had done the same on the telephone. Both had found a persistent press on both ends with questions about Hattie. Their refuge had been discovered! She and Josh had been forced to move to another suite.

Bea was thoroughly pissed. Hattie's drama had not only messed with her love life but with the roof over her head. It had to come to an end!

As Connie sat listening to Bea trying to placate Hattie's kids, Connie was thinking the same thing as her friend. Too much drama was going on, and it had gotten out of hand. All she had wanted to do on this trip was have a good time with her friends, nothing more. Hattie had upset those plans and interfered with her time with David. Something had to give because she had made all of the compromising she intended to make. When Bea disconnected the call from Hattie's children, Connie let her know exactly what was on her mind.

"I love Hattie, but I'm sick and tired of this, Bea. She has all but ruined the last part of this trip for all of us."

Bea didn't disagree. She knew where this was leading. "We've got to make a decision. Either one of us stays with her until this is all worked out…"

"Or we all get on that plane tomorrow and let the chips fall where they may," Bea finished.

The two friends looked at each other in unspoken agreement. Both knew the choice that they planned to make, even friendship had its boundaries.

****

Hattie sat in the crowded holding cell rejuvenated as she sang the hymn "Onward Christian Soldiers" to the top of her lungs. From the heckling that she was receiving from fellow cellmates she knew that her solo wasn't appreciated. Yet, even the threats of the officers to extend her charges to disturbing the peace didn't deter her from her exuberant performance. Hattie really didn't care what anybody thought. She was feeling good. At the bail hearing she had taken her stand and she was raising her voice in praise whether they liked it or not!

Why shouldn't she? The small courtroom had been packed with her supporters. Reverend Trees and Vivian Journal had seen to that. The group was so vocal that their fervent Hallelujahs and Amens had the judge threatening to toss them out of court. One insulted believer hollered out how the Lord would smite him if he tried. The judge was as good as his word and tossed her out before returning his attention to Hattie and her attorney.

"How do you plea?"

"Sin is taking over Las Vegas, your honor, and the Lord's Word is needed here—badly," Hattie responded passionately. "I wouldn't have done my Christian duty if I hadn't tried to do something about it. So I'm taking a stand on the side of the Lord and I plead that his will be done."

Her supporters went crazy, whooping and hollering. Once again the judge called for order before looking down at her sternly.

"I'll ask one more time, Mrs. Collier, how do you plead?"

Hattie's attorney, Roger Sherman, was one of the top counselors in Las Vegas. He issued a warning in Hattie's ear and she got the message.

"I plead not guilty," she answered, but she still had a message of her own. "I am guilty of nothing except love, your Honor."

Her supporters shouted their approval. A gentle nudge in her side from her attorney reminded Hattie what was at stake. She refrained from saying anything else.

Flashing a disapproving look Hattie's way, the judge studied some documents before him before speaking. "Bail is set at $50,000. See the bailiff on your way out."

Roger thanked the judge and started to usher Hattie out of the court room, amid the jubilant cheering of her supporters, but she shrugged him off and addressed the judge.

"Surely you're not saying that I have to pay $50,000? I don't have that kind of money!"

"Only a portion has to be paid," Roger assured her. Then he whispered, "Don't worry, Josh said that he'd cover the bail."

"No he won't!" she told him. "I'm not paying it and he's not paying it either." Hattie was adamant. She addressed the judge. "I won't pay a dime!"

Roger looked shocked and apologized profusely to the judge as Hattie flopped down in her chair, gripped the sides and began to sing the song, "I Shall Not Be Moved." Her supporters began to chant her name. Chaos erupted in the courtroom.

The judge rocketed from his chair and shouted, "We'll just see about that. Bail is denied! Bailiff, escort this woman from the court room!"

With the shouts of praise and support ringing in her ears, the bailiff had pried Hattie out of the chair and had led her from the court. A short while later she had been tossed back in jail with the harlots.

Hattie wasn't oblivious to her plight. She could actually go to prison in this sin filled city so far away from home. If she did, it could be years before she saw her children again and she would miss her grandchildren growing up. The thought of that saddened her. What a sacrifice that would be, but throughout history Christians had been martyred for their religious conviction. She would simply be among the number.

Looking around at her fellow inmates she noted that they were the same ones that had been in there a few hours ago before her hearing, but her two protectors of earlier were gone.

"Where are Janet and Renee?" Hattie asked Christina, who was still there and as sullen as before.

"What am I, the zoo keeper?" She sneered.

Hattie eyes narrowed and she was about to give Little Miss Smart Mouth a piece of her mind when one of the other inmates spoke up.

"They took the lesbos to their bail hearing."

"Lesbos?" Hattie wasn't familiar with the term.

Christina snorted loudly. "Lesbos, lady! Women who sleep together! Homos!" She threw her hands up in the air in frustration. "Lord! How dumb can you get?"

Although stunned by the revelation Hattie still managed to nail Christina on her wording.

"So I see that you do know how to call on the Lord."

The young woman seemed surprised by Hattie's retort. Realizing that Hattie would twist anything that she said, she decided not to get into a verbal fight. Withdrawing, Christina, walked to the other side of the cell and sat on the floor as she ignored the taunts of the other women who were glad to see her get bested.

Hattie was about to follow her when an officer called her name for the second time that day. She acknowledged her presence.

"You've got visitors," he said roughly, then unlocked the cell. "Come with me."

Bea and Connie were waiting for her in the stark grey room used for visiting. To her delight, Reverend Trees was with them.

He stood to greet her when she entered. The smile on his face told her how glad he was to see her. The smile that she gave him in return said the same. As they stood grinning at each other, it seemed that the other people in the room were forgotten. Connie cleared her throat to get their attention.

"Hattie could you and the reverend stop giving each other goo-goo eyes and sit down. We've got some serious business to discuss here and not a lot of time to discuss it."

"You've got that right," Bea added. The look on her face and on Connie's didn't match the one on Reverend Trees'

Hattie sat down and the reverend reached across the table and took her hand.

"We're all praying for you," he informed her softly. "What you're doing takes a lot of courage."

"Oh really?" Bea raised a sculptured brow. "Well, I think it takes a lot of foolish behavior to throw Bibles on people's heads and then refuse bail when the court is good enough to offer it to you. Josh was nice enough to get his friend to act as your attorney and you do something like this. You would think that you would be grateful!"

"Ain't it the truth!" Connie snapped.

"Refusing bail, indeed!" The more Bea thought about Hattie's selfishness the madder she got. Pushing away from the table she started to rise and pace, but the look from the guard stopped her. Settling back at the table, she leaned into Hattie. "We leave for home tomorrow and we plan to get on that plane with or without you. Your attorney was prepared to get court permission for you to go with us..."

"I didn't know that," Hattie answered defiantly, determined that they weren't about to make her feel guilty.

"Well you blew it!" Connie was feeling just as frustrated as Bea. "On top of that you've got those people out there on the street acting crazy. Somebody can get hurt."

"That's not going to happen." The reverend spoke up. "They're down there in support of what Hattie is doing."

"Maybe the ones you brought," Bea challenged. "But you can't tell me that the APES, and the AASSes are out there for the same purpose."

"To say nothing of those other nuts marching around carrying signs," added Connie.

"You can't blame Hattie for all of those people!" The reverend puffed up like he was about to deliver a sermon.

"Yes we can!" Bea and Connie bellowed simultaneously.

Both stared the minister down. It looked as though the three of them might come to blows when Hattie spoke up.

"I appreciate all of your concerns but I've got faith that everything will turn out fine." She paused as the three of them deflated. "By the way, where is Miss Fanny?" She hadn't been in court, nor had she come to visit.

Eyes began to shift and look at everything in the room except her.

"She's around," Connie answered.

"Yeah, she's doing her bit," Bea generalized.

"I'm sure that she's concerned like the rest of us," The reverend replied.

"In other words, she didn't consider my plight important enough to stop gambling." Hattie concluded. She knew how to read between the lines. "And don't tell me that she's not."

Pounding a fist on the table, she elicited a warning look from the guard. "See, that's the reason that I've done all of this and that I'm staying in here. This place will turn an eighty something year old woman living off of Social Security and a pension into a gambling fiend. That woman can't afford to be losing money. She's got bills to pay. Now the Lord sent me to Las Vegas for a reason…"

"Uh huh, and I know exactly what it was." Bea interrupted as her eyes slid to the reverend then back to Hattie.

Hattie's mouth tightened around the edges as she warmed in embarrassment while silently having murderous thoughts about her best friend. It was the reverend who salvaged the moment.

"I think that your cause is a noble one, Hattie, and I'm proud of you." He turned to Bea and Connie. "If you ladies are her friends you'll try to see that she acted unselfishly for what she believed in. This is her future at stake not just vacation plans." He squeezed Hattie's hand and she returned the gesture.

"Excuse me, but can we dispense with the romance for a minute," Bea barked at Hattie. "You've interrupted my chance to get me a bit of loving because every time I turn around I'm being dragged somewhere because of you and your stupid Bible stunt." She snatched Hattie's hand from that of Reverend Trees. "So no touchy feely on my watch."

Connie rose to leave. "We love you, Hattie, but tomorrow we're out of here."

Bea followed suit. "You want to be a martyr, you've got it."

Both of the women stalked to the door. Hattie wanted to feel badly about what was happening, but her cause was righteous. She couldn't give in. The reverend rose to leave as well, but the message that he delivered was a much different one.

"Hattie, I'll be staying right here in Las Vegas. We're going to resolve this." Leaning across the table, he planted a soft kiss on her lips.

Back in the cell, Hattie brushed her fingers gently across her mouth. She could still feel the taste of him as she stared dreamily through the bars at the dull, grey wall beyond. It was plastered with wanted posters hanging in disarray. She noted that one of the photos looked familiar, but that wasn't what was on her mind. She was wondering if Reverend Trees' resolve to stay by her side was the beginning of everything that she had imagined when she had decided to pursue him. If so, the Lord had answered her prayer. All she had to do now was wait this Bible tossing charge out, and get out of jail so that she could see in which direction the relationship with the reverend would lead.

CHAPTER 19

Hattie tried to ignore the noisy chatter around her in the semi-crowded cell. So many things were swirling in her head. What if she didn't beat the rap? She quickly dismissed that thought. She had been trying to do the work of the Lord and he was on her side. She didn't know that those itty bitty Bibles could do any damage or injure anyone. At least no one had been hurt. She comforted herself with a prayer of thanksgiving, but that was short-lived when she thought about her so-called friends.

The heifers were going to leave her to rot in jail. On top of that her mother-in-law was in the troughs of gambling addiction. Only Reverend Trees remained faithful to her, and that really mattered. Although her reason for wanting to come to Las Vegas might not have been the most righteous, God had seen fit to give her another purpose and she was grateful.

Hattie stood to stretch. She then wandered over to where Christina sat huddled alone in a corner of the cell.

"Have you given any thought to turning you life around?" Hattie asked giving her a hopeful look.

"Have you given any thought to minding your own business?" Christina retorted.

Hattie tried a different tactic. "How do you like living out here in Sin City? I bet you've seen some strange things."

"You don't know the half of it, lady." Christina looked at Hattie for a moment and there was that flash of fear in her eyes that Hattie had noticed before.

There was a long silence between the two women as once again Christina erected the invisible wall between them. Hattie watched the young girl thoughtfully as she began to bite her fingernails. Hattie chuckled.

"Who are you laughing at?" the girl challenged.

Hattie smiled. "You made me think of my granddaughter. She bites her nails like that when she's worried or frightened."

"Really?" Christina's tone dripped with sarcasm.

"Yes, really." Hattie gestured to the young prostitutes hands. "I've notice that you've practically chewed your nails to your fingers which means something must really be bothering you. So I want you to know that God watches over us even when you're alone, sitting in a jail cell."

Christina gave a troubled sigh, and then suddenly the cold indifference that she had exuded since Hattie had met her seemed to visibly melt away. She looked around to see if anyone else was close enough to hear what she was about to say. Satisfied that there was sufficient distance from the others, she leaned toward Hattie.

"I have seen a lot since I've been in Vegas, but nothing like what I saw a few nights ago."

Sitting down beside her, Hattie urged her on. "I'm listening,"

Studying the older woman for a moment to judge whether she could trust her, Christina made a decision. She whispered.

"I was on the street the other night when a guy came walking toward me. I thought he might be a trick so I…"

"Trick?" Hattie was momentarily confused.

"You know a John, a Trick." Christina snapped. "A business customer."

"Oh." For a split second she almost asked who John Trick was, but she stopped herself.

Exasperated, Christina rolled her eyes and continued. "Anyway, I was pouring it on because I really needed the money and this jerk waves me off. He seemed like he was in a big hurry, but he kept looking over his shoulder. Well, I'm thinking that meant that he wanted me to follow him. So, I look around for the cops and didn't see none, and when I turned back around in his direction, just that quick, the man was gone.

I knew that he couldn't have reached the corner. I mean, no one could walk that fast. So I started walking that way, you know, to see if I could find him. When I came to this alley between two buildings I could hear a kind of grunting noise, and some scuffling like somebody was fighting. I stayed hid and peeked around the building..." Christina's voice trailed off and she started biting her nails again. This time the fear in her eyes was raw.

Hattie put a consoling arm around her shoulder. "What did you see?"

Christina didn't shrug her off, but seemed to be emboldened by her effort to comfort.

"I-I-I saw a large man choking the john to the ground. A streetlight was shining into the alley and I could see him real good. The guy on the ground was fighting but after a while he was still. I was scared to death. I had to put my hands over my mouth to keep from screaming, but he must have sensed me or heard me or something. He looked up and looked straight at me. Lady, I ran like I never have before. I don't know if he got a really good look at me, but he did see me and I saw his face!"

The urgency in Christina's whisper caused other inmates to look over at the two of them huddled together. Hattie continued to console the girl.

"Did you go to the police?"

Christina gave a disgusted snort. "Are you kidding? You know what I do for a living? Me and the cops ain't exactly buddies. All I did was try to stay out of sight after that. I laid low for a day, but I needed money so I waited until the next night and went out again. I was so scared. I kept thinking how would I know that the next guy that picked me up wouldn't be the one who killed that man and what was stopping him from killing me?"

Hattie recoiled at the thought. "So how did you end up in here?"

"I have a gift for spotting the vice cops," she said with pride. "I walked around until I spotted a guy that had cop written all over him. I went right up to him, offered my services and just like that I was arrested. I'm thinking I'm safer in here than on the street."

Hattie was at a total loss for words as she tried to absorb the girl's tale. "You have got to tell the police. I'll tell them for you if you want." She started to rise, but Christina pulled her down.

"No! Don't say a word," Christina was frantic. "I don't have money for bail so I'll spend a few days here. By then, he might have moved on. Look, maybe I'm just paranoid. Maybe he's forgotten all about me." She sounded doubtful.

"Collier!"

Hattie jumped when she heard her name called. "Yes?"

"More visitors," the officer who had called informed her.

Hattie gave Christina a reassuring pat on her hand. "Don't worry, child. I'm going to pray for you and you'll get through this."

Hattie found herself back in the same room where she had visited earlier with Bea, Connie and Reverend Trees. This time it was Hattie's attorney occupying the room and Reverend Trees was with him. When she saw the reverend Hattie beamed like a school girl, but there was hardly time for them to greet each other before the attorney got straight to the point.

"I've got good news for you, Mrs. Collier." Roger Sherman informed her.

Hattie held her breath. "Yes?"

"Well, I believe that I can talk the DA into reducing your charge and we can get you out of here for good, possibly with probation."

Hattie frowned. "I don't like it.

"You don't like it?" The attorney and the reverend spoke simultaneously. Both of them looked at her as if she had lost her mind.

"No I don't," explained Hattie. "It sounds like I'm pleading guilty to something and all I was doing was trying to keep a whole lot of people from causing a bottleneck at the gates of hell. I didn't know the Bibles would cause any damage and I didn't know that pilot was drunk, so I plead the fifth."

The attorney sighed patiently. "Mrs. Collier, there is nothing for you to plead the fifth about. The police arrested you at the airport. The pilot named you as the one who hired him and you admitted it. Case closed."

"Hattie, I admire you for standing on your principles," Reverend Trees interjected. "I want you to know that the people at the Convention are backing you all the way. But I'm asking you to take the plea. The thought of you spending another minute in this place is too hard. Please, I'm begging you, follow Mr. Sherman's advice."

Hattie heard the worry in the reverend's voice and she had to admit that although she was strong in her conviction, she wasn't thoroughly convinced that part of God's plan for her was to languish in a Las Vegas prison. Squaring her shoulders, she made the attorney a proposal.

"Listen, Mr. Sherman, I'll consider what you said on one condition. There's a young girl in the cell with me, barely out of her teens that's been making a living out here as a street walker. I want you to talk to her and see if you can help her."

The attorney looked uncomfortable with the request. "Mrs. Collier, I don't mind representing you since you're Josh's friend and while I appreciate your sympathy for lost causes, I don't think…"

"I know that I'm not paying you for representing me, so I can hardly ask you to take time with somebody like Christina, but this is not about prostitution—wrong as that is. This girl needs help. She's seen something that she needs to tell the police about and she needs an attorney. Make arrangements to help her and you can get me out of your hair."

"Are you saying that if I do this, you might leave Las Vegas, for good?" The attorney didn't try to hide his look of relief.

Hattie nodded. "If they let me go, that's exactly what I'm saying."

Standing, Roger Sherman closed his leather brief case, straightened his silk tie and called for the guard to open the door. Before he hurried out of the room he turned to Hattie. "What's her last name?" She told him.

After he left, Reverend Trees turned to Hattie. "I guess that means he's going to help her."

Hattie grinned. "I made him a deal that he couldn't refuse."

****

"I've got nothing else to say!" Christina cried in protest. "You people are gonna get me killed." She looked accusingly from Hattie to Roger Sherman and finally at Detective Norwalsky who was also in the room.

"This is not an inquisition Christina," Norwalsky tried to reassure her. The expression on her face showed that she thought that was a lie.

Norwalsky continued. "You're an intelligent woman. You could do anything you want if given the opportunity and we can offer that. We discovered the body of the man that you saw murdered the other day. He was a drug trafficker. While no one here is going to mourn his death, there have been a string of murders that are associated with a drug cartel that we want to bust."

"If my client can identify the killer we want all charges against her dropped," Roger interjected. It had been he who had convened all of the principals in the room in what seemed like record time. He had heard Christina's story and had also agreed to represent the girl for free.

"In addition, since her life may be in danger she'll need protection and a safe haven."

"Well let's see if she can identify him first," said Norwalsky. He placed yet another mug book in front of Christina. This was the third one that she had looked through.

Hattie sat silently, listening. She was here at Christina's request for moral support and to reiterate what the young woman had told her about what she had seen.

As Christina reviewed the pictures, Norwalsky left the room to get some coffee while Mr. Sherman stepped out the door to talk to the guard who had escorted Hattie and Christina to the room in which they were meeting. Restless, Hattie decided to get up and stretch. Slowly she wandered around the room, gazing at the posters. The wall was full of them. She made mental observations about the exploits of each wanted person. Her heart was full of sorrow for the victims of these lost souls.

One particular poster caught her attention and she stared at the face quizzically. There was something about the man that looked familiar. But how was that possible? She didn't know any criminals. She moved on.

Suddenly, Hattie stopped as a memory tried to push its way to the forefront. It was something about one of those posters. She had observed a duplicate one of them on the wall outside of the holding cell. She worked her way backward as she reviewed the wanted poster that had caught her eye.

Mr. Sherman stepped back into the room, followed by Norwalsky who checked on Christina's progress.

"Any luck?"he asked.

Christina's eyes were locked on the book. Suddenly she jabbed at a photo with her forefinger.

"That's him!" Christina and Hattie said simultaneously.

All eyes turned to Hattie as she stood mesmerized staring at one of the wanted posters. A large man with a thick brown mane streaked with gray stared back at her with menacing green eyes.

"That's him," both women announced again as they referenced different pictures.

Norwalsky looked down at the person Christina had identified then looked up at the poster that Hattie had spotted. He looked over at Roger Sherman.

"It's the same man!" He returned his attention to Hattie. "Mrs. Collier, I don't understand. How could you possibly know this man?"

Across the room, Roger answered for Hattie. "At this time Mrs. Collier has nothing else to say. Mrs. Collier, please remain silent."

"Why would I do that? I've got nothing to hide." Hattie was excited at the prospect of helping to catch a killer.

"Mrs. Collier, please!" Roger pleaded. "We should talk first."

Norwalsky smiled as he guided Hattie to a chair next to Christina. He propped his large frame on the corner of the table at which they were sitting and glared at both of them. He didn't look happy.

"Now ladies, I don't know what's going on here, but we're trying to gather evidence on a murder case. I don't appreciate my time being wasted like this."

"What do you mean wasted?" Hattie was indignant. "Christina said that she saw that man over there on that poster kill somebody, and I'm telling you that I've seen him too!" She jabbed at the picture in the book.

Norwalsky looked at them smugly. "That's highly unlikely, ladies, since I know for a fact that the man that you're identifying was found dead a few months ago in a downtown hotel." Ripping the poster from the wall he growled, "Do you want to try again?"

Hattie was adamant. "Dead my foot! He couldn't be dead when I saw him less than a week ago."

"Are you sure Mrs. Collier?" asked Roger. He had given up on trying to silence her.

"Of course I'm sure."

"And what about the fact that I saw him kill a man just two nights ago?" Christina added.

Noting the look of certainty on the faces of the two women, Norwalsky seemed less sure of himself. He leaned into Hattie. "Okay, just what do you know about this man?"

Hattie relished the moment. "I don't know anything about him. All I know is where he was when I saw him." She gloated as everyone looked at her expectantly. "He was in that sinner's den, The Love Goddess."

She went on to recount how she had been unceremoniously tossed out of Larry Smith's establishment when "green eyes" was coming in the back door.

The doubt that Norwalsky had displayed seemed to be fading. He looked hopeful.

"I don't know how it's possible, but it's something that we can look into. We've been trying to tie Smith and this guy together for a while, but Smith's been too slick, and when we found that body our case against him went nowhere. So ladies, I'm going to ask you one more time are you absolutely certain that you've seen the man in this picture and on that poster alive in Las Vegas this week?"

For a third time the two women answered simultaneously. "Yes!"

A smile graced Norwalsky's face. "Then, I think that we've might have killed two birds with one stone."

CHAPTER 20

Hattie couldn't believe what was happening. Was this a trick? She'd seen things like this on television when they took the prisoner out of jail in the middle of the night, put them in a car and took them to some unknown destination without telling them why. Usually those types of stories ended in disaster—incarceration in a horrible prison, or even death! She gulped. Oh, Lord! Was that going to happen to her?

After the session yesterday with Mr. Sherman and the detective, Christina and she had been put in separate holding cells. Hattie wasn't familiar with any of the new faces with whom she shared the cell, but they were still the same assortment of streetwalkers, petty thieves and women who had hooked up with the wrong man and had found themselves on the wrong side of the law. Immediately, Hattie had gone about providing the unfortunate sinners with the Word.

Planting herself firmly in the middle of the cell, Hattie didn't try the individual approach this time. She went straight to reading aloud from the Bible. She quoted the verses that told about the Lord's displeasure with harlots, but she let them know that they could be redeemed. As in the previous cell, her efforts hadn't been received as graciously as she had hoped. Although the women were as diverse as their crimes they were united in their curses and cries for her to cease and desist.

Hattie had remained stalwart in spite of their threats. She had been sent to Las Vegas on a mission from an authority higher than mankind. However, eventually she did temper her fervor. She reduced her efforts to the humming of her favorite spirituals. Eventually one of the harlots, most of whom had been avoiding her like the plague, sidled up to her.

"You that Bible Bomber?" She looked at Hattie from beneath false eye lashes so long that they looked like spiders sitting on her face.

"I don't like that word, bomber used with the word Bible," Hattie sniffed. "All I did was share the word of the Lord and I'm being crucified like Jesus."

"Well I heard on the street that you're costing the casino owners on the Strip a fortune. Folks are staying away from there because of all of the holy rollers that came here to march for you. They're prowling around the Strip passing out all kinds of religious crap making the gamblers nervous. Even us hoes is losing money. I had to get arrested so I could get me three square meals and a bed for the night. The customers are tip-toeing around us like they scared of going to hell or something."

"Thank you, Jesus!" Hattie rejoiced. That was the best news she had heard in days. "My work has not been in vain."

"Lady, you the devil's helper," the woman hissed. "Why don't you go back where you came from and leave us honest working girls alone."

As she watched the woman drift back to the other side of the jail cell, Hattie's spirits had lifted. Only moments ago, she had been feeling desperate and down hearted at her inability to get anybody interested in hearing the word of the Lord, but now she knew that she had made an impact. Sinners were being saved. The surge of pride that she felt couldn't be described.

The following morning when she awakened, Hattie was stiff from having been forced to recline on one of those awful uncomfortable cots. While most of the other detainees had been either released or hauled away, Hattie was still in the holding cell. But she felt good—that is until the police officer called her name.

She had answered and followed him as ordered. Detective Norwalsky was waiting for her in the hallway. To her surprise he and some other officers escorted her into a service elevator that took them down into a basement garage where a squad car with tinted windows was waiting. Norwalsky ignored Hattie's questions about where they were going, and that's when she grew concerned. This didn't look good, but at least she hadn't been handcuffed like some sort of criminal.

Once again she demanded, "Where are you taking me? I want to know this instant! I want to call my attorney!" She didn't mean to sound scared or desperate, but the truth was that she was both.

They whisked her out of the garage through the back of the building. She could hear the distant sound of the protestors in the front of the building calling for her freedom. If she hadn't been hemmed in between two burly officers she would have made a break for it and dashed toward her supporters screaming for help. Instead she decided on another course of action.

Detective Norwalsky was sitting in the front passenger seat. Leaning forward, Hattie blew in the detective's ear.

"What the hell!" He whipped around and gave her an evil glare. The officers on either side restrained her.

"What did you do that for? I could hold you for assaulting an officer!" Norwalsky sounded as shocked as he looked as he jiggled his finger in his ear.

Hattie crossed her arms haughtily. "Oh, so you can talk. I was beginning to wonder. So where are you taking me?"

"You'll see when we get there," Norwalsky snapped.

It was obvious to Hattie that she would get nothing further from the stubborn detective so she did what she had to do. Squaring her shoulders and clutching her Bible, she decided that if her Jesus had to suffer for what he believed so could she. Let that Pontius Pilate Norwalsky take her out somewhere and nail her to a cross. She could take it. There was a Power higher than the Las Vegas Police Department on her side. She began to sing "Onward Christian Soldiers," ignoring the threats of officers to handcuff her and gag her, or even worse, throw her out of the moving car.

The sighs of relief were audible when they reached their destination. By that time she had serenaded them with two additional spirituals, tossing in a high spirited sermon asking for the redemption of their souls. When they came to a stop, the officer driving the car told Norwalsky that he was putting in papers for "hazardous" duty when they got back to the station.

As they exited the car, Hattie noticed that they were at a small airport. Colorful, air craft dotted the field, along with a multitude of hangers. It reminded her of the airport where she had met the pilot who dropped the Bibles, only this one was upscale.

"What are we doing here?" She asked.

As was the pattern, no one answered. Surrounded by the officers, she was lead into a small brick terminal and to her surprise and relief Bea, Connie, Miss Fanny, Josh, David and Reverend Trees were all there. Tears of joy burned Hattie's eyes as they gathered around her, greeting her happily.

"We're going home!" Bea said as she hugged Hattie.

Connie added, "All of us, including you!"

Hattie pulled back. "What do you mean?"

"You're free!" Reverend Trees smiled broadly.

"You're a hero!" said Miss Fanny, who had been playing a slot machine when Hattie entered. Abandoning it, she joined the gathering. "They're flying us out of here in style by private jet! All of our bags are aboard the plane and the pilot is waiting."

Hattie frowned in confusion. "What is everybody talking about?"

As if on cue, a winded Roger Sherman breezed through the doors that led out onto the tarmac. Walking briskly, he was waving a handful of papers.

"Good, you're here, Mrs. Collier! I've got all of the paperwork signed assuring your release and you and your friends can be out of here shortly."

"Okay," Hattie answered with uncertainty. "But what papers?"

Her attorney looked taken aback. "Don't you know what's happened? Hasn't anybody told you?"

"No! Nobody's told me a thing!" Hattie's voice rose in frustration. Had everybody in this town lost their minds!

Roger fixed Norwalsky with an accusing stare. The husky officer gave a nonchalant shrug.

"She's your problem now, counselor. I was told to get the woman down here to the airport. I did what I was supposed to do."

Norwalsky motioned the accompanying officers toward the exit. He started to follow them, but Sherman caught his arm.

"I think the least that you could do is tell the lady what happened and thank her. You owe her that much."

Norwalsky shot him a threatening look, but the attorney, although half his height and weight, was not intimidated. The haggard detective expelled an aggravated sigh. All he wanted to do was leave this batty woman behind and go home. Yet, despite all of the trouble that Hattie Collier had been to the Department he couldn't deny that Sherman was right. He did owe her an explanation. He turned to a frowning Hattie, who glared at him suspiciously.

"Have a seat please." He gestured toward one of the brightly colored chairs lining the small waiting room.

"No thank you." Hattie replied tightly. "I can hear what you have to say standing up." This man had made her time in Las Vegas miserable. She wasn't going to make anything easy for this ward of the devil.

"Okay then." He looked at the spectators gathered around Hattie and then returned his attention to her. "After you and Christina told us about Omen Carmelli…"

"Who is Omen Carmelli?" asked Hattie.

"The guy that you and Christina identified yesterday," Norwalsky explained. "The one that we thought was dead."

"Thought was dead? So you did find out that he was alive, huh?" Hattie wanted to shout Hallelujah. The truth had come to light.

"Yes, we did." Norwalsky knew that behind her question was the need for an apology from him. He planned on giving it to her in time, if she'd just let him finish what he had to say.

"Again, after you two ladies identified Carmelli, based on that information I went and got a search warrant for Larry Smith's place. It turned out to be the perfect storm. He didn't expect us and was totally unprepared for... "

"I don't know why he shouldn't have expected you. All of the shameful activity going on in that den from hell, you would…"

"Hattie! Would you let the man finish," Bea snapped.

Irritated at being chastised, Hattie rolled her eyes at Bea. "Go ahead and tell the story," she directed.

Norwalsky gave Bea a grateful glance before continuing. "Anyway, it turns out that Smith and Carmelli are more than partners in crime. They're lovers."

"Do, Jesus!" Hattie's eyes widened.

"They're obsessed with each other. It was Smith who identified the badly disfigured body that we found in that hotel. Supposedly some members of a rival drug cartel killed Carmelli. The body was burnt beyond recognition. The teeth had been knocked out and the hands were cut off."

Hattie and the others cringed at the description of the brutality that the officer described. Norwalsky continued.

"It was all a trick devised by Carmelli and Smith to fool the cartel. We should have checked the DNA, but we didn't. We were just glad to get rid of him. That was a big mistake. So after you and the girl identified Carmelli, our plan was to take Smith in for questioning. Something unsavory is always going on at The Love Goddess so we raided the place and detained the patrons. Two of our officers were sent to secure the alley to make sure that nobody took that way out, and lo and behold, who do they find sneaking out of the back exit big as you please but Omen Carmelli. He was so sure that we weren't looking for him that he didn't even have on a disguise, just a hat."

"So the dead can rise again," Hattie quipped.

"Yes, in this case. We found a hideout that Smith had made for him in the attic of his club. Carmelli had been hiding out at Smith's place until arrangements could be made to get them both out of the country. The man that Carmelli killed was a hit man from an opposing cartel. It seemed that there was a hit out on Smith, but Carmelli got the assassin first."

Connie was curious, "If Carmelli is alive whose body did you find in the hotel?"

Norwalsky shrugged. "We're trying to identify him; but with Christina's testimony, there should be a lot of arrests and cases solved because of this bust. It was quite a coup for the precinct thanks to you and the young lady, and we're grateful."

Norwalsky figured that he could afford to be a little humble. Not only had they caught Omen Carmelli, but it was icing on the cake being able to catch Larry Smith. Harboring a fugitive and complicity in a murder were the least of the charges that they would be levying against him. There was no doubt that the resulting action would be plenty of citations and a couple of promotions.

"Think nothing of it, Detective," Hattie sensed how hard it was for a man like him to say thank you. "The Lord had his hand in this every step of the way. Christina and me were just his workers. And speaking of Christina, where is she? Ya'll didn't throw her in prison did you?"

"No, she's our star witness against Carmelli. She's off the street and in our witness protection program. She'll get moved out of Las Vegas, provided with a place to stay, a job and a new chance in life."

"Praise Jesus!" That was the best news she had heard in days. "The Lord does work in mysterious ways."

"Tell the truth!" Miss Fanny testified.

"All charges have been dropped against you," Roger informed Hattie, "and there's a private plane out there on that tarmac that is going to fly you and your friends back home."

"Josh's friend provided his private jet!" Bev piped in, grinning at him proudly

"He's the CEO of one of the hotel casinos on the Strip," Josh explained.

"Oh really." Hattie raised a brow. "So I guess he's anxious to get me out of town too."

"What do you mean, Hattie?" Reverend Trees looked at her confused.

"I mean that I heard that the work that we did for the Lord in this town was not in vain, Samuel. We gave those sinners the Word and so many of them followed it that some of the casinos on that Strip have fallen on hard time!"

"Thank you, Lord!" Reverend Trees raised his hands in praise before hugging Hattie.

"Is that true, Detective?' Bea addressed Norwalsky.

The detective looked like a deer caught in a pair of headlights. His Captain had called him this morning demanding that he get Hattie Collier out of Las Vegas and be quick about it. She and her Bible thumping cohorts were costing the city a fortune and the powers that be wanted her gone.

"You don't have to be shy about it," Hattie smirked. "It can't be much of a secret. I found out about it from a prostitute in the lock up."

"I don't care who, what, why or where," said Miss Fanny. "If we're going home on a private luxury jet, let's go!" She started toward the exit leading to the airstrip.

"I'm with Miss Fanny," said Connie. Hand in hand with David she followed after her.

"Me too," Bea chirped happily. Las Vegas had been the experience of a lifetime, but it was time to go. She and Josh thanked Roger and fell in step behind Connie and David.

Hattie pumped the hand of the hard working attorney. "I'm grateful, Mr. Sherman. You'll be in my prayers."

He smiled. "Thank you, Mrs. Collier. I need all of the prayers that I can get."

Hattie grabbed Reverend Trees' hand. "Come on, let's get on that plane." He didn't move. She turned to him expectantly.

"I'm not going with you, Hattie. I've got some things to do to close out the convention. I'll be flying back home the day after tomorrow."

Hattie was disappointed, but she put on a brave face. "All right, I know that you've got to finish the Lord's work. But, I guess my own is done here, even if all of the Bibles weren't given away."

Reverend Trees took her hands in his and pressed them to his heart. "Listen to you, dedicated to the last. You're the best woman I know, Hattie. But don't worry about the Bibles. They were all given away."

Hattie's eyes widened. "Really!"

"Absolutely. With all of the people in town we couldn't miss the chance to see that they got the Word, too. We gave away the rest of them to some of the people in the groups that demonstrated. Lord knows that there were members of the APES, and the AASSes that could use them."

Hattie couldn't disagree with that, and the reverend didn't give her time to do so as he drew her to him and kissed her.

"I'm going to miss you," she confessed when they parted.

"I'm going to miss you too." He planted a kiss on her temple. "Now go before your friends come back in here and drag you away. They're waiting."

With a final wave goodbye, she started toward the exit doors. On the way she passed Miss Fanny, who had stopped at a slot machine to play one last time before leaving.

"Miss Fanny, you're supposed to be out there on the plane." Hattie was disgusted. It looked like the biggest sinner in Las Vegas lived in her own home. "Get off of that thing and let's go."

"Shoot!" Miss Fanny glowered at the one arm bandit. "I'm through with this town. I haven't won a thing in three days!"

"It serves you right, you old back-slider. You're not getting any sympathy from me."

Hattie held the door for her while Fanny tore herself away from the slot machine. Pulling the arm one last time, she slid from the stool and walked toward her daughter-in-law. It was the bells, whistles, lights and music that halted her steps.

Miss Fanny turned back to the machine. Numbers were spinning like crazy. The red light on the top was flashing in a circular motion. The policemen and Mr. Sherman had left. Except for the two women, Reverend Trees and an attendant at the snack bar, the building was empty; but everyone present rushed to the slot machine and watched in wonder as the amount of money that she had won began to mount.

They stood opened mouthed when the figure stopped at two million dollars and the bells and whistles stopped. Hattie's knees nearly gave way. Reverend Trees had to keep her from falling to the floor. There was bedlam among the small group of witnesses as they screamed, jumped up and down and hugged each other in celebration of Miss Fanny's good fortune. It was the grand prize winner herself who found the words to sum up seven days in Las Vegas that wouldn't easily be forgotten.

"Hallelujah!" She screamed doing a jig that belied her age. "Sin City is all right with me!"

THE END

ABOUT THE AUTHORS:

L. Barnett Evans is a novelist, playwright, and award-winning storyteller. She has given spoken-word performances at schools, churches, art festivals and various other venues across the country. She has written several plays: *Is God Calling My Name?, North Star*, and *The Body of Christ*. She has also written for newspapers and magazines. Her novel, *And All the People Said...*is a suspense thriller. Her comedy fiction, *Grandmothers, Incorporated* was her first collaborative effort and was co-written with C. V. Rhodes. Barnett Evans also collaborated with Rhodes on the play, *Grandmothers, Incorporated* which enjoyed a successful Off-Broadway run. Barnett Evans holds a Bachelor degree in Business Administration. Visit her website at: www.lilliebarnettevans.com

C. V. Rhodes is an author and an award-winning playwright. She is the author of six published romance novels. Her titles include: *Sin, Sweet Sacrifice, Sinful Intentions, Singing a Song..., Small Sensations*, and *Still Waters....* Her comedy fiction, novel, *Grandmothers, Incorporated*, co-written with L. Barnett Evans, was selected as Best Book of the Year by two online websites. Written Word Magazine named Rhodes as one of the Ten Up and Coming Authors in the Midwest. As a playwright she has been the recipient of the BTA Award for the Best Original Writing for her stage play, *Stoops*. Rhodes holds a Master degree in Sociology and has written for newspapers magazines, radio and television. Visit her website at www.crystalrhodes.com

Visit the authors' website at:

www.grandmothersinc.com

Novels by

L. Barnett Evans and C.V. Rhodes

Grandmothers, Incorporated
Saving Sin City

Available in Ebook format at Amazon.com

****

COMING SOON!

Grandmothers Incorporated Adventure #3

She's so sweet and she's so kind, but...

SOMETHING IS WRONG WITH MISS ZELDA

Made in the USA
Middletown, DE
17 February 2019